THE HIDDEN WINDOW MYSTERY

A magazine article offering a large reward to anyone who can find a missing medieval stained-glass window intrigues Nancy. She asks Bess and George to join her on a search in Charlottesville, Virginia. Before the three friends leave River Heights, their adversary tries to get them to postpone the trip. But no luck. Nancy is determined to carry through her plans.

During the girls' investigation of old southern mansions, they encounter a ghost who turns the tables and makes them disappear. Eerie sounds come from a beautiful estate that is surrounded by a high brick wall. Why will the owner allow no one to enter?

How Nancy solves these mysteries and locates the stained-glass window will keep the readers on edge for many hours.

The ghost!

NANCY DREW MYSTERY STORIES

The Hidden
Window Mystery

BY CAROLYN KEENE

PUBLISHERS   *Grosset & Dunlap*   NEW YORK

Contents

The Hidden
Window Mystery

CHAPTER I

The Peacock Mystery

"GOOD-BY, Hannah!" said Nancy Drew. She hugged the motherly, middle-aged housekeeper, then put a hand on the front-door knob.

"Watch out for falling tree branches," Hannah Gruen warned the attractive reddish-blond-haired girl. "This is the worst April wind I've ever seen. We should have had it last month. March is the time for high winds."

Outside, there was a continuous roar. But above the din, Nancy and Mrs. Gruen heard a loud crash on the front porch.

"What was that?" Hannah asked, worried.

Nancy yanked the door open. "Oh!" she exclaimed.

Lying in a heap near the edge of the porch was their letter carrier, Mr. Ritter. He was unconscious. His bag had tumbled down the steps, and letters, newspapers, and magazines were flying about.

Nancy and Hannah rushed to the man's side. He had evidently hit his head, for there was a large red mark on his temple. They lifted the victim gently and carried him into the living room.

"Maybe we'd better call a doctor," Nancy suggested.

Mr. Ritter's eyelids flickered. In a short while the sixty-year-old letter carrier regained consciousness and refused medical assistance.

"I'll be all right in a minute, but I'd appreciate it if you'd bring in my mailbag. By the way, Nancy, there's something in it you'll be mighty interested in."

The young girl hurried from the house. Her blue eyes sparkling in anticipation, she began to gather the letters, newspapers, and magazines that were being swirled across the neighboring lawns by the strong winds. It took Nancy nearly ten minutes to collect the mail.

She entered the living room with the mailbag slung over her shoulder. She was glad to see Mr. Ritter sitting up in a chair and drinking a cup of tea.

"Oh, thank you, Nancy," the letter carrier said. "It was mighty careless of me to stumble and knock myself out. That wind is fierce. It blew some dirt into my eye, and for a moment I couldn't see where I was going."

"How do you feel?" Nancy asked gently.

Mr. Ritter declared he would be ready to resume his deliveries in a few minutes. "I'd like to finish my tea before I face the blustery weather."

"May I help you sort the mail?" Nancy offered. "And what was it you wanted to show me?"

As Mr. Ritter began rummaging in the bag, he said, "I read an article in a magazine telling about a large reward. It's being offered to anyone who can solve the mystery of a missing stained-glass window."

Nancy was intrigued at once. "What magazine was the article in?" she asked eagerly.

Mr. Ritter pulled a torn, soiled copy of the *Continental* from his bag. "This is for your new neighbor, Mrs. Dondo."

Nancy said she did not know the woman.

"I'm sure she won't mind if you look at the article," the letter carrier said. "You're a good amateur detective, Nancy, and if you can solve this one, you'll certainly put another feather in your cap."

Nancy smiled and began to read. Sir Richard Greystone of England was trying to trace a medieval stained-glass window that had been in his family since the fourteenth century. He believed the window had been brought to the United

States about 1850, but all trace of it had been lost. Sir Richard was offering a large reward for any information leading to its whereabouts.

The article went on to describe the window, which pictured a knight riding off to battle. The family shield he was holding had a peacock emblazoned on it.

Nancy's eyes danced with excitement. "Thank you, Mr. Ritter, for telling me about this," she said. "Is there time for Hannah to read the article?"

The letter carrier said a few minutes more before getting back to delivering the mail would not matter.

When the housekeeper finished reading, she looked puzzled. "A peacock on the shield, eh?" she said. "You know some folks think peacocks, especially the feathers in their fantails, bring bad luck."

"But I know you don't believe that," Nancy declared.

"Those marks in the fan," the housekeeper stated, "are said to be evil eyes." She looked at Nancy affectionately. "But I always taught you not to be superstitious."

Hannah Gruen had lived with the Drews and taken care of Nancy ever since the girl's mother had passed away fifteen years ago, when Nancy was three years old.

*"A reward for anyone who can solve the mystery of
a missing stained-glass window,"* Mr. Ritter said.

Nancy remarked that in India peacocks are held to be sacred.

"That's right," Mr. Ritter agreed. "And so are the cow and the monkey."

The letter carrier stood up and announced that he felt well enough to return to his delivery route. "I'm already late," he said. "Folks will be wondering what's happened to their mail."

He thanked Nancy and Hannah for their assistance, then started for the door, accompanied by the others. As he reached it, the bell rang and someone began pounding loudly on the door.

When Mr. Ritter opened it, Nancy and Hannah saw a strange woman standing there. Her bleached blond hair, blown by the wind, stuck out straight from her head. She was short and sallow-complexioned. Her dark eyes blazed.

"How do you do, Mrs. Dondo," said the letter carrier. "I'd like you to meet your neighbors, Nancy Drew and Hannah Gruen."

The woman did not acknowledge the greeting, and ignored Nancy and Hannah. Waving a fist at Mr. Ritter, she said, "I saw what was going on. You've been taking time out in this house. Do you realize how long you've been here? Why aren't you on the job?"

Nancy and the others were so startled by the woman's irate manner that they stood open-mouthed.

"Listen here, Mr. Ritter," the woman went on,

"you've got some mail for me, and I want it right away. There's an important letter I have to have and you've been dillydallying all this time. Give it to me at once!"

Mrs. Dondo pushed her way into the hall and leaned over the mailbag. She put her hand in to grab a letter, but Mr. Ritter told her he would tend to this himself. Quickly he went over every piece of mail in his pouch.

"There's nothing for you today, Mrs. Dondo, except a magazine," he said. He handed the *Continental* to her.

"And what a mess it is!" she shouted. "More of your carelessness. And don't tell me there wasn't a letter for me. It was in your bag before you let the mail blow all over the neighborhood. You'd better find it too! That letter had a hundred dollars in it, and I don't propose to lose it!"

"A hundred dollars!" Mr. Ritter cried out, a look of alarm coming over his face.

"Yes, a hundred dollars!" Mrs. Dondo repeated. "And if you've lost that letter, you're going to pay me the money yourself!"

CHAPTER II

An Unpleasant Neighbor

FOR a moment Nancy thought Mr. Ritter would collapse; he was so upset.

"Mrs. Dondo," she asked, "do you have any proof that the letter was in this particular delivery?"

"You keep out of this," the woman said, glaring at the young girl. "I'll handle the matter in my own way."

"I doubt that you could make any claim," Nancy went on, despite the rebuff.

"I'll get proof and I'll see that I get paid!" Mrs. Dondo screamed. "I'll carry this story to the postmaster!"

Hannah Gruen stepped forward. "But right now you'll get out of this house," she said firmly.

With an angry shrug the unpleasant woman turned and left. Nancy asked Mr. Ritter where she lived.

"Down near the corner," he replied.

Nancy offered to search further for Mrs. Dondo's letter or any others she might have missed. From the time Nancy had discovered *The Secret of the Old Clock* up to the young detective's latest adventure, *The Witch Tree Symbol*, she had been helping people, often exposing herself to grave danger.

"My little terrier, Togo, is good at finding things," Nancy told the letter carrier. "I'll get him to help me."

She urged Mr. Ritter not to be too concerned about Mrs. Dondo's accusation. They both knew it was illegal to send cash through the mail.

The letter carrier said he was still worried. Even though the woman could not collect the money from him or the postal authorities, a complaint to the postmaster for carelessness would be a black mark on his record.

"And I'm near retirement age," he added. "I'd like to leave this job with a clean slate."

"You will," Nancy said, smiling at him affectionately.

After Mr. Ritter had gone, the young sleuth hurried to the kitchen, where Togo was taking a nap. "Before I go shopping, pal," she said, "we have a job to do. Come with me."

The little dog jumped up, cocked his head, and followed his mistress into the front hall. She was showing him a white envelope when the telephone rang. The caller was Bess Marvin, one of Nancy's two best friends.

"What's new?" Bess asked.

"A couple of mysteries. Why don't you and George come over and I'll tell you all about them?"

"Sounds like fun. We'll be right there."

George Fayne and Bess Marvin were cousins. George, in keeping with her boyish name, wore her dark hair short and preferred sporty clothes. Bess, in contrast, was very feminine and chose to dress along those lines. She was blond and slightly overweight because of her fondness for rich food.

Nancy went outside to wait for the girls, who arrived in exactly ten minutes.

"Hypers, Nancy," said George, "you hardly give us time to recover from one mystery before you have another to solve. What's going on now?"

Nancy laughed. Then, sobering, she quickly explained the need for a further hunt for Mrs. Dondo's letter.

When she finished, Bess said, "I've heard Mother speak of Mrs. Dondo. She says the woman is a troublemaker."

George warned, "You'd better be careful, Nancy."

"In what way is she a troublemaker?" Nancy asked.

Bess said that Mrs. Dondo had come from Virginia. "She left there because of some unpleasantness with her neighbors. At least, that's what Mother heard at a club meeting."

"What was the matter with her?" George demanded.

Bess said Mrs. Dondo was a social climber, a schemer, and a very unpopular person. "She isn't a bit like other people in this neighborhood," Bess went on. "I can't understand why she came here."

Meanwhile, Togo had been crawling under the hedges and foundation plantings of nearby homes, sniffing for envelopes like the one his mistress had shown him. While waiting for the girls, Nancy had been looking in the trees and high bushes. Neither she nor the dog had had any luck.

Bess and George eagerly joined the search and for nearly a half hour the group combed the entire area thoroughly.

Finally Bess sighed. "If there were ever any letters around here, they're gone now. Maybe other neighbors found them."

"That's very possible," Nancy agreed. She said that since all the families in the neighborhood were fine people, they would have delivered any mail they found to the addressees.

"Then maybe Mrs. Dondo has her letter by now," George suggested. "Let's find out."

"And if she doesn't," said Nancy, "I'll try talk-

ing her out of going to the postmaster. I'd hate
to see Mr. Ritter get into trouble. He's been a
wonderful friend to all of the people on his
route."

The three girls walked to the Dondo house.
Before they had a chance to ring the bell, sounds
of quarreling voices came from the open window.
A man, whom the girls assumed to be Mr. Dondo,
was reprimanding the woman.

"That was a pretty cheap trick of yours, trying
to get easy money out of the mailman."

The woman flared in reply. "What do you
know about it?"

"I know this much," the man replied. "That
good-for-nothing brother of yours, Alonzo, would
never send you a hundred dollars."

"Oh, be quiet!" Mrs. Dondo screamed. "Alonzo
is all right. You just don't like him."

"You bet I don't like him, and for good reason,
too. Alonzo's too slick for his own good. If he
ever told you he was sending you a hundred dollars, he sure was kidding you."

When Mrs. Dondo would not admit that her
husband was right, he said, "I don't like your
brother's business dealings, but I don't think
he's stupid. Alonzo wouldn't send that much cash
through the mail."

The three girls looked at one another and
smiled. Nancy had never picked up such incrimi-
nating information just by accidental eavesdrop-

ping! She and her friends tiptoed away and hurried back with Togo to the Drews'.

"Mrs. Dondo may still try to make trouble for Mr. Ritter," said Bess, as they went inside.

"Let her try it!" George said with disgust. "Nancy, Bess told me that you had two cases to solve. What's the other one?"

Nancy smiled. "The three of us are going to hunt for a stained-glass window."

"What!" the cousins chorused.

Quickly Nancy explained about the article in the *Continental* and the reward offered to anyone finding the old window that pictured the knight with the peacock shield.

George looked interested, then grinned. With a twinkle in her eye, she asked, "Nancy, what'll you do with all that money? You may ruin your amateur standing as a detective."

Nancy quickly explained that she would not take the money for herself. "I've been thinking I'd love to make a donation to the Hospital Fund —toward the new children's wing. If I win the reward money, it can be paid directly to the hospital."

"That sounds wonderful," said Bess.

"Will you help me?" Nancy asked the cousins. "Then we can make the donation together."

George agreed at once, but Bess said one angle of the mystery worried her. She was seated in a large upholstered chair in the living room, near the doorway into the hall. Now she pulled her feet up under her and propped her chin on one fist. "I don't like this peacock business."

"Don't tell me you're superstitious about peacocks!" George teased.

"You know better than that," Bess said. She turned to Nancy and asked, "Have you any theory as to what happened to the stained-glass window?"

"No," the young sleuth replied. "Of course the window may have been destroyed long ago, but I'm hoping it hasn't been."

"It could have been taken down and stored away," George said. "People sometimes get tired of looking at stained-glass windows and remove them, just as they do pictures."

"The place where the window was may have changed owners several times," Bess said. "They may have had a lot of hard luck and blamed it on those evil eyes in the peacock's fan."

"Oh, Bess," said George, "you always——"

The words were hardly spoken when a terrific bang startled Nancy and her friends. The next moment a gust of wind blew into the room, carrying with it a large peacock feather, which came to rest at Bess's feet! The girl shrieked.

CHAPTER III

A Plea for Help

FOR a few tense seconds the girls did not move. Bess was too terrified, George and Nancy too startled.

Then Nancy sprang from her chair and dashed into the hall. Wind roared through the wide-open front door. She slammed it shut and looked around, wondering where the peacock feather had come from.

"Hannah!" Nancy exclaimed. The housekeeper was descending the steps, a bunch of peacock feathers in one hand!

By this time Bess and George had reached the hall. They looked at Hannah in amazement.

"Where did you find those feathers?" Bess asked.

"After talking with Nancy, I remembered these in the attic," Hannah explained. "They belonged to her grandmother."

Mrs. Gruen laid the peacock feathers on a table in the living room and the girls examined them closely.

"Aren't they beautiful?" Nancy remarked. "I understand the formation of the eyes in the feathers is one of the most unusual things in nature."

"Indeed it is," said Hannah, "and the bird is very proud of its feathers. Remember that old expression 'proud as a peacock'?"

When the girls nodded, the housekeeper continued, "It comes from the fact that a peacock greatly values his fan. It's said that when his tail feathers are plucked to be sold, the bird is so ashamed he hides for days. He won't eat and sometimes mourns his loss until he dies of starvation."

"Oh, how awful!" Bess remarked.

Just then the girls heard a key in the front door, and Mr. Drew came inside. A tall, handsome man, Nancy's father practiced law in River Heights.

"Hi, Dad," the young detective said, hurrying to kiss him.

He greeted the others, then asked Nancy, "Do I detect a gleam in those blue eyes that means you're involved in another mystery?"

Nancy smiled and told her father about Mr. Ritter's accident and Mrs. Dondo's accusation.

"That's too bad," the lawyer commented.

When Mr. Drew had settled in his favorite chair, Nancy recounted the story of the missing stained-glass window.

"That's very interesting," said Mr. Drew when she finished, "but tracing a window lost since eighteen fifty will require considerable investigation."

"But it'll be fun," Nancy added.

"I have a client who is an authority on stained-glass windows. He may be able to help you," the lawyer continued. "Mr. Atwater is retired now and not in the best of health, but he loves to talk about his art. Perhaps I can make an appointment for you to see him tomorrow. It's Saturday and he may not be busy."

"I'd like to go along," George suggested.

"Me, too," Bess added. "Does your friend still make stained-glass windows, Mr. Drew?"

"Yes, but only as a hobby. He has a very complete studio in his home."

Mr. Drew went to the telephone. A few minutes later he returned to say that the girls had an appointment at ten o'clock the next morning.

The following day Nancy picked up Bess and George in her convertible. Fifteen minutes later, they arrived at Mr. Atwater's home. As Nancy parked, a tall, slender man with white hair came out of the small house.

"How do you do," said Nancy, smiling. "Are you Mr. Atwater?"

"I certainly am," the man replied. "You're right on time, Miss Drew. I recognized you from the picture on your dad's desk."

Nancy introduced her friends, and then the artist led the way inside his studio. The place was extremely neat. Rows of tools hung above a workbench. A drawing table and a cutting bench were arranged along another wall.

Mr. Atwater invited the girls to sit down. "Your father mentioned a mystery in connection with your visit here, Nancy."

"Yes, there is one I'd like to solve." She told him about the window Sir Richard Greystone was eager to find.

The artist smiled. "I'll do everything I can to help you locate it."

Nancy thanked him and said, "I presume that if the window is still in existence, its colors are very lovely. I understand that modern stained-glass windows don't have the same striking effect as those of the middle ages."

Mr. Atwater nodded. "That is true. The old-time glass had many imperfections—for example, there were bubbles in it. But these very weaknesses have given the windows their lovely satiny appearance."

"How are modern stained-glass windows made?" George asked.

"Well," said Mr. Atwater, "I'll try to give you a brief description. First, I would take measurements and ascertain the direction of the light and the amount that would fall on the window in its future setting."

"Is that so you would know how much depth of color to use?" Nancy questioned.

"Exactly," Mr. Atwater said. "Next, I'd make a small-sized sketch of the picture I would color and enlarge into a working drawing, called a cartoon. Then it would be marked up to show the actual size, shape, and color of each piece of glass.

"Transparent paper would be laid over the drawing and the design copied exactly. Then I'd cut this paper along the dividing lines, and I'd have a pattern for each piece of glass."

"When do you cut the glass?" Bess asked.

"That's the next step. I lay the pattern pieces on sheets of glass in the colors I want and cut them out. When they're ready, I assemble my colored-glass picture on a large plain sheet of glass and fasten it down with molten beeswax."

He glanced at a saucepan on top of the stove. "I was just melting some before you came. My picture is now fitted into a frame, and black lines, representing the leading between the pieces of glass, are painted on. Then, by holding the picture up to the light, I can get the over-all effect of color and design before adding the details of the picture, which I paint in by hand."

"My," said Bess, "it certainly is complicated."

"Yes," Nancy agreed. She noticed that the

elderly man's face showed signs of weariness. "I'm afraid we've been so interested that we didn't realize how much time had passed. Perhaps we can come back again."

The man admitted he was tired, but urged the girls to pay him another visit soon. They thanked Mr. Atwater and got up to leave.

As George went toward the door, one foot skidded. In trying to keep her balance, she clutched wildly at a table on which there was a sharp piece of plate glass.

"Oh!" she exclaimed, as blood spurted from a deep cut on the palm of her right hand.

Mr. Atwater sprang to George's side. "I'm dreadfully sorry," he said. "It's my fault. I must have spilled some beeswax on the floor."

The artist hurried to a first-aid kit hanging on the wall and opened it. After thoroughly cleansing the wound on George's hand, he deftly bandaged it. During the treatment he apologized profusely.

"It's nothing," George insisted. "The cut will soon heal."

Nancy remembered what her father had said about the elderly man's health. "Perhaps you should rest now," she suggested.

"I will," he promised, "but first let me give you a catalog. It contains a list of all the prominent firms and individuals who make stained-glass windows," he added, handing her the booklet.

Nancy thanked him and the three girls returned to their homes. After lunch the young detective studied the catalog. She turned page after page. None yielded a clue to the missing window.

Just as Nancy reached the W's in the alphabetical list, Hannah asked, "Have you had any luck?"

"Not until this very minute," the girl replied. "You brought it to me."

The housekeeper looked over Nancy's shoulder and read:

> WAVERLY STUDIO
> Mark Bradshaw, Owner
> Charlottesville, Va.

"Charlottesville!" Nancy exclaimed. "That whole area was settled by English people. It's a perfect place to look for the Greystones' stained-glass window."

"Do you think Mr. Brawshaw might know something about it?" Hannah queried.

"I hope so," Nancy replied. "What's more, Charlottesville is where my cousin Susan Carr lives. She's often invited Bess, George, and me to visit her."

"I know Susan and her husband Cliff would love to have you. Why don't you call them?" Hannah suggested.

"A good idea," Nancy agreed. She dialed the

number, and Susan answered. She said she would be delighted to have the girls stay with them.

"You'll just adore it, Nance. Our garden is perfectly beautiful now. It's going to be open to the public during Garden Week."

"How wonderful, Sue!" said Nancy. Then she told her cousin about the stained-glass-window mystery.

"Sounds as if you're coming to the right place to look for it," Susan agreed. She wanted them to meet the new friends that the Carrs had made during the two years they had lived in Virginia.

"Fine," Nancy replied. "Good-by for now."

She called Bess and George and told them her plans. They agreed enthusiastically. She had just put the phone down when it rang. She answered.

"Nancy, this is Mr. Ritter." The letter carrier's voice was strained. "Something terrible has happened. I need your help at once!"

CHAPTER IV

A Puzzling Telegram

"I'LL be glad to help you if I can," Nancy told Mr. Ritter.

"When I went to Mrs. Dondo's this morning," the letter carrier explained, "she showed me a special-delivery letter from her brother. He said he had sent her a hundred-dollar bill that she should have received by now. Mrs. Dondo is still accusing me of stealing it and insists she is going to discuss the matter with the postal authorities!"

Nancy was alarmed. Even if Mrs. Dondo could not prove her case, she could make it so unpleasant for Mr. Ritter that other people on his route might lose confidence in him.

"I'll certainly do what I can for you," Nancy promised. "Let's call on her right away."

"I'll come over to your house."

Mr. Ritter arrived in a short time, and together

they walked to the Dondo home. The disagreeable woman opened the door.

"So you've brought your detective with you, I see," she said acidly. "Well, that's okay with me. Come in and I'll show her the letter from my brother."

Nancy and Mr. Ritter followed Mrs. Dondo into the living room. She opened a desk drawer and took out a letter that she handed to the young girl.

Nancy glanced at the postmark. It was stamped Charlottesville, Virginia, the day before! In the left-hand corner was the sender's name—Alonzo Rugby. But there was no return address.

The contents of the letter confirmed Mrs. Dondo's story. Short and to the point, it read:

> *Dear Sis,*
> *Like you asked me on the phone*
> *I am writing this to tell you that*
> *I did send you a hundred-dollar*
> *bill in a letter a few days ago.*
> *You should have received it on*
> *Friday.*
>
> > *Your loving brother,*
> > *Alonzo*

Nancy glanced up. Mrs. Dondo was staring at her with narrowed eyes. "Now I guess you're convinced," she said. "But if you think I'm going to let Mr. Ritter get away with my hundred-dollar bill, you're very much mistaken."

"I want to tell you something, Mrs. Dondo. I have known Mr. Ritter a long time. He is an honest man. It is most unfortunate that the letter was lost, but as I said yesterday, your brother should never have sent cash through the mail. It's illegal."

Mrs. Dondo's eyes flashed. "I don't want your advice, young lady! Maybe you're right after all about Mr. Ritter. You're the one who went around picking up the letters. I'm beginning to think you kept the money!"

Nancy was furious. "Mrs. Dondo, your statements are ridiculous and you know it. You haven't lived here long. But you'll find people in this neighborhood are friendly and honest. They're not suspicious of one another. I suggest that you drop this whole matter at once or you may find living here very unpleasant."

Mrs. Dondo was taken aback for a moment but quickly recovered. "I've got a good family too. My brother is a talented artist. Neighbors or no neighbors, I don't intend to be talked out of getting my hundred dollars back." She went to the front door and opened it. "Good-by."

Outside, Nancy told the letter carrier, "I'll tell my father about this latest development and he can take care of everything. Incidentally, I'm going away on a short trip."

When she told him that her destination was Charlottesville and that she would look up

Alonzo Rugby, Mr. Ritter smiled for the first time. "You're a good friend, Nancy," he said. "Thanks a lot."

As soon as Nancy reached home, she telephoned her father and gave him all the details. He promised to watch out for Mr. Ritter's interest should the need arise.

Nancy now packed her clothes for the upcoming trip. As she closed the suitcase, she decided to write a letter to Ned Nickerson at Emerson College. They had been friends for several years.

"It would be nice if Ned could come down to Charlottesville while I'm there," Nancy thought, as she picked up her pen.

After telling Ned the news and how she hoped to find the missing stained-glass window, Nancy gave him Susan Carr's address. When she finished the letter, she posted it at the corner mailbox.

As Nancy walked back to her house, Togo came bounding down the street toward his mistress. In his mouth was a small piece of paper. Nancy leaned over and tried to take it from him.

"So you're not going to give it up." She laughed as the terrier pranced around.

The game went on for several minutes. Then Togo, apparently deciding to do something else, let Nancy take the paper. It was part of an envelope. On it was a canceled stamp and the postmark was Charlottesville, Virginia, three days before!

"Togo, where did you get this?"

The dog barked excitedly but made no move to show her. A frightening thought occurred to Nancy. Suppose, when Togo had been looking for the missing letters the previous day, he had found the one with the hundred-dollar bill and torn it to pieces!

Worried, she took the dog into the house and told Hannah her fears. "Now I'll really have to solve that mystery," she said. "Maybe the Drew family does owe Mrs. Dondo a hundred dollars!"

"I might believe that if you hadn't overheard what Mr. Dondo said to his wife," Hannah replied. "I'm inclined to think that woman is faking the whole thing.

When Mr. Drew returned that evening, he handed Nancy three plane tickets. "You'll fly to Richmond tomorrow morning and then go from there by car to Charlottesville."

Nancy called Bess and George. "Dad and I will pick you up right after church," she said.

The next morning, shortly after breakfast, the telephone rang. Nancy answered it.

"Miss Nancy Drew?" a woman asked.

"Yes."

"This is Western Union. I have a telegram for you from Charlottesville, Virginia. It's signed Susan Carr. The message reads: 'Postpone your trip. Will write when convenient for you to visit.'"

Nancy could not believe that Susan would send such an ungracious message! She repeated the telegram to her father.

"Maybe something unexpected happened," Mr. Drew said.

"I suppose I could start to hunt for the stained-glass window somewhere else," Nancy declared. "But I would still like to talk to Mr. Bradshaw, who makes stained-glass windows in Charlottesville."

"Why don't you go anyway and stay at a hotel," Mr. Drew suggested.

"I'll call Bess and George and see if that will be all right with them," Nancy replied.

The cousins agreed to the new arrangements and Nancy reminded them, "Dad and I will pick you up as scheduled."

Mr. Drew drove the girls to the airport and they had a smooth flight to Richmond. The threesome claimed their luggage and taxied to the Hotel Richmond.

"What a lovely city!" Bess remarked, as they drove through the tree-lined streets and saw one charming colonial house after another, each with a beautiful garden.

When the travelers were settled in their spacious room, George turned on the television for the latest news. The local station was broadcasting. Suddenly the girls were electrified by an announcement.

"While driving to the Richmond airport, Mrs. Clifford Carr of Charlottesville was sideswiped by another car, and she overturned in a ditch. She was taken to Johnston Willis Hospital. There is no trace of the driver who caused the accident."

"Oh, my goodness!" Nancy cried out. "That's Sue! We must get to the hospital at once. I hope she's not seriously hurt."

The girls put on their coats and hurried outside, where they hailed a taxi. The driver's slow pace taxed their patience but finally they arrived at the hospital.

Nancy led the way inside to the desk and said to the woman in charge, "We'd like to see Mrs. Susan Carr."

The woman gave the room number and the girls went upstairs. They found Susan, pale and wan, lying with her eyes closed. A second later the girl awoke.

"Nancy!" she cried out. "I'm so glad you're here. But how did you learn about the accident?"

Nancy told her about the news broadcast. "You're probably surprised that we came after you sent the telegram."

"I didn't send you a telegram!"

Nancy glanced at Bess and George. All three knew now that someone had tried to keep Nancy from coming to Charlottesville.

Another thought occurred to Nancy. Perhaps the same person, knowing the telegram ruse had failed, had also sideswiped Susan's car, hoping to keep Susan from meeting the girls! But what was the reason for keeping them apart?

Nancy hoped to learn more details. She said, "Sue, your accident might have some bearing on the telegram. Do you think the person who sideswiped you did it on purpose?"

"Oh, yes," Susan replied. "There was no one on the road and the man had lots of room to pass. He came up alongside me so close that I was forced to the side of the road. The next thing I knew I went into the ditch and turned over. And the man never stopped to help me."

"Did you get a good look at the driver?" Nancy asked her cousin.

Susan shuddered. "He had a horrible and unnatural face. He probably wore a stocking over his head."

"Have the police been notified?"

"Yes."

"Then, promise me you'll try to get some sleep now. How long does the doctor think you'll have to stay here?"

"Oh, I can go home tomorrow. My car will be fixed by that time." Susan looked at Nancy affectionately. "I'm so glad you came. My husband is away until tomorrow. I'll get a good night's sleep and we'll start for Charlottesville in the morning."

The travelers said good-by and went back to

the hotel. The rest of the afternoon and evening was spent in viewing the old city with its many historic spots, including the courthouse designed by Thomas Jefferson and old St. John's Church, where Patrick Henry delivered his immortal "Give me liberty or give me death" oration.

As the girls were ready to tumble into bed, Bess remarked with a yawn, "I feel as if I'd had a refresher course in American History!"

After breakfast the next morning Nancy called the hospital and talked with Susan, who felt much better. She asked Nancy to pick up her car at the Blossom Garage and then come to the hospital.

"Of course," said Nancy. "See you soon."

The owner of the Blossom Garage, a pleasant young man, said the girls could take the car. After paying the bill, Nancy drove to the hospital. Susan was waiting. She slid into the seat alongside the driver. George and Bess were in the back.

About five miles out of town, as they started around a curve, Nancy found that the steering apparatus would not work. The wheel spun around wildly. Frantically she jammed on the brakes, but could not regain control of the car.

The vehicle plunged into an embankment!

CHAPTER V

Telltale Magazine

THE car's passengers were thrown forward by the impact. Nancy braced herself against the steering wheel. Bess and George fell to the floor, not injured. Susan, however, had been flung hard against the windshield, and she blacked out!

Nancy leaned over and eased Susan back onto the seat. "We must get her to a doctor!" she exclaimed. "I think we passed a physician's home and office about a quarter of a mile back."

"I'll go," George offered, and started off.

Nancy and Bess watched Susan closely. Presently the girl's eyelids flickered open. "Where am I?" she asked, dazed.

"We had a little accident," Nancy replied in a soothing tone. "George has gone for a doctor. Just lie still, Sue."

In a short time George and Dr. Steyer arrived. Nodding to the others, he examined the patient.

"This young lady will be all right," he said. "She's had a bad shock, but nothing's broken. I suggest that you all come to my office while we see what can be done about your car."

The girls accepted, and Dr. Steyer helped transfer the luggage to his automobile. "As soon as we reach my office, I'll call a service garage," he offered.

When the mechanic arrived, Nancy rode with him to Susan's car and told him that she suspected the steering mechanism had been improperly repaired after the accident the day before.

"I'll soon find out," the young man said. After checking the car, he reported that either the steering assembly had not been tested or it had been tampered with later.

"In any case, the car's in bad shape. You won't be able to drive it until the grill and front wheels are straightened and a whole new steering assembly is put in."

Nancy asked the mechanic to tow the car to his garage and make the necessary repairs. He agreed and then drove her back to Dr. Steyer's office.

When Nancy told the others of the mechanic's report, Susan became very upset and began to cry hysterically. Dr. Steyer gave her a sedative and in a few minutes she went to sleep.

"She'll wake up in about an hour, feeling a lot steadier," he said.

Mrs. Steyer now came in from shopping. When

she heard the story, she offered to drive them to Susan's home.

"I was planning to go to Charlottesville this afternoon," she said, "and I'd like company. Please have some lunch with the doctor and me and then we'll leave."

The girls accepted her kindness. While the meal was being prepared, Nancy telephoned the Blossom Garage in Richmond and spoke to the owner.

After hearing her story of the morning's accident, the man referred to his records and reported, "The steering assembly of that car was checked and was in perfect condition."

"What do you think happened?" Nancy asked.

The man said his watchman had reported hearing muffled hammering and had glimpsed a prowler leaving the garage the previous night. "I'm guessing, but maybe that fellow damaged your car."

Nancy hung up. She felt sure the man's surmise was correct. If Susan had no enemies, it seemed obvious that the strange man was trying to injure Nancy, Bess, and George.

"Someone wants to keep us away from Charlottesville," she told herself. "But why?"

The thought that Alonzo Rugby might be responsible went through her mind, but Nancy dismissed it at once. The loss of a hundred dollars was not provocation for such drastic retaliation!

"Whoever the person is, he must be desperate," she realized.

Susan awoke just as lunch was ready and apologized for the way she had acted. "I guess two accidents were two too many," she said.

After lunch, the group set off for Charlottesville. As they entered the town, Mrs. Steyer asked, "Where do you live, Susan?"

The young woman gave directions. Her home, Seven Oaks, was about three miles out of town. When they reached it, Nancy, Bess, and George gazed at it in delight. A low brick wall ran across the front of the small estate. An iron gateway opened onto a tree-shaded drive with beautiful, flower gardens on either side of it.

Facing the end of the drive was a white clapboard two-story colonial house. At the entrance was a small porch with Doric columns. Above this was a balcony, which Susan said opened off her bedroom.

"It's perfectly charming!" Nancy exclaimed.

The girls thanked Mrs. Steyer and walked toward the house. The front door was opened by a plump, smiling housekeeper.

"Land sakes, Miss Susan!" she cried. "It's mighty good to see you walking around."

"And I'm glad to *be* walking around," Susan replied. "Anna, our guests are Nancy Drew, Bess Marvin, and George Fayne."

"Now don't you worry none about the luggage," Anna said as the girls reached for their suitcases. "I'll have them to your rooms in a jiffy."

She picked up all three suitcases at once and went up the stairs with them. Susan showed the visitors their three adjoining bedrooms, papered in dainty colonial patterns, each with a fireplace.

Susan said she would meet the threesome downstairs after they had unpacked and changed their clothes. By the time Nancy, Bess, and George returned to the first floor, Susan's sandy-haired, six-foot husband had arrived.

"You girls have come at the right time," he said. "There's a neighborhood mystery to be solved."

"Not another!" George groaned.

Cliff laughed. "Susan told me about the stained-glass window and the fake telegram," he remarked. "But surely you can add one more to the list."

"Tell me what the mystery is," Nancy begged.

"We have a neighbor named Mr. Honsho, from India. A couple of years ago he bought one of the most beautiful old estates around here."

"It's called Cumberland Manor," Susan said. "Mr. Honsho spoiled it by putting a high wall around the grounds, and no one has been allowed inside since!"

Cliff took up the story. "Nancy, strange sounds come from the place day and night. And well— the fact is—we want you to solve the mystery."

"And for a very special reason," Susan continued. "Before Mr. Honsho bought the place, it was always open to the public during Garden Week. We'd like you to find out what those horrible screeches are, stop them, and persuade the owner to permit visitors."

"A big assignment," George remarked.

"Yes, it is," Cliff said. "Some of the men around Charlottesville have tried, and the Garden Tour group too. But so far we've failed."

"Well, count me out," Bess spoke up. "I'll help with something that's not so weird."

"Then suppose you take over the case of Mrs. Dondo's brother," Nancy suggested, her eyes twinkling mischievously.

"No, thank you," Bess answered quickly. "If any men are coming into my life, I want them to be young and handsome. I don't think any brother of hers could meet either of those requirements." The others laughed.

When Nancy said she wanted to go to Mr. Bradshaw's studio the next day, Cliff offered to lend the girls his station wagon. "I won't need it. Why don't you visit Bradshaw after you see Mr. Honsho? The two places aren't far apart. They're both on Eddy Run, which is a creek that flows past the rear of the properties."

The three girls started off after breakfast the following morning. On reaching Mr. Honsho's estate, they gazed at the high brick wall and the solid-iron entrance gate, which completely screened even a glimpse of the interior. Nancy noticed a bell at the side of the gate, stopped the car, and got out to ring it. There was no answer.

"I'd say Mr. Honsho just doesn't want visitors," Bess remarked.

Nancy was reluctant to give up so easily. She drove to the point where the brick wall turned toward Eddy Run, and stopped. "Let's walk down alongside the wall," she urged. "We may come to another entrance."

She and the cousins followed a dirt path that skirted the enclosure. Bicycle tire tracks were evident, and a few minutes later the girls saw a young man on a bicycle stopping at a high wooden door. He dismounted and took a key from his pocket.

Nancy ran forward and came close enough to attract his attention. He looked up at her in surprise. About twenty-five years of age, he was slender with reddish hair. He wore a work shirt, jeans, and a cowboy belt.

"Please wait!" Nancy cried out.

The young man paid no attention. He opened the door, shoved his bicycle inside, and slammed the door. Bess and George reached Nancy just as the lock clicked.

"I wonder who he is," George said.

"He must work at Cumberland Manor," Nancy

"I wonder who he is," George said.

remarked. "Probably he's been told not to talk to strangers."

Suddenly, from inside the estate came a horrible screech. Then there was an ominous silence.

Bess cowered against the other girls. "Somebody's being tortured in there!"

"If so," Nancy said, "we must try to help the person!"

"But how," Bess questioned, "when we can't even get inside the place?"

Nancy was stymied. The screech had sounded somewhat like a screaming tomcat, but more foreboding.

"I believe I know what that sound may have been," she said. "A peacock!"

"What makes you think so?" George asked.

Nancy explained that she had read a lot about peacocks after she had decided to look for the old stained-glass window. "From the description of the bird's screech, it would sound like that."

Bess, who was not convinced, thought they should report the matter to the police. "I'm going back to the car," she declared.

Nancy and George wanted to do some more sleuthing. They continued along the path, which led all the way to Eddy Run. To their disappointment, the brick wall was as high across the water side of Cumberland Manor as the section they had just seen. It contained no opening. Finally they gave up and returned to the car.

On the way to Mr. Bradshaw's studio, they passed another estate. Apparently it had once been an attractive place, but now it showed signs of neglect.

"There's the name," said Bess. "Ivy Hall."

About half a mile beyond was the entrance to Waverly. A roadway wound among well-kept lawns and fields. As they neared a rambling farmhouse, Nancy spotted a sign with an arrow that indicated Mark Bradshaw's studio was at the rear of the property.

Nancy continued down a lane. To the left of it were lovely flower gardens and to the right a dense woods. A short distance from Eddy Run and standing under the branches of a giant spreading oak was the studio. It was a long, brick building almost completely covered with English ivy.

As Nancy parked, the studio door opened. A thin man in his late forties, wearing a smock and horn-rimmed glasses, came outside.

"How do you do," he said in a low vibrant voice.

After introductions, Nancy told him they were interested in stained-glass windows, and had learned a little about the art from Mr. Atwater, who had a studio near them in River Heights.

Mr. Bradshaw invited them into the studio. "Is there something in particular you wish to know?"

Quickly Nancy explained about the article in *Continental* and asked if he had heard about it.

When he said no, she gave him the details. Then she added that Susan Carr had suggested they come to him.

"The Carrs are very nice people and I would certainly like to help you," the artist said.

"Perhaps you could tell us where some of the famous works of stained-glass art are located in this area," Nancy suggested.

Mr. Bradshaw shook his head. "I'm sorry, but I'm not too well versed on that. But I would be glad to tell you about the art itself. The more you know of the process, the better able you'll be to recognize the genuine article if you find it.

"Actually, a stained-glass window is a translucent mosaic held together by lead. But the lead between the sections is not just a fancy glue. It plays a real part in the design."

"The leading is almost the last thing that is done, isn't it?" Nancy asked.

"Almost," the man replied. "The final step is the cementing, which holds the leading and the glass together."

"Would you mind explaining the cutting table, Mr. Bradshaw?" George requested.

"Why, certainly," the artist said. He led the way to one of two benches, which stood at the far end of the room. Each was solidly built and had a thick plate-glass top. "This," he explained, ensures a constantly flat surface, which is of utmost importance in the cutting process."

Beneath it a large mirror was tilted diagonally from the front edge of the table to the back of a shelf below. A brilliant light on the mirror was helpful to the cutter when he worked with dark glass.

"And this," said Mr. Bradshaw, picking up an odd-looking tool, "is a wheel glass cutter. The square-grooved sections have the funny name of nibbling mouths."

As he was speaking, Nancy caught sight of a magazine carelessly thrown behind one of the benches. The advertisement on the back was the same as that on the copy of *Continental* she had seen.

Unnoticed by the others, she slid her foot under the bench and flipped the magazine over. It was the issue of the magazine that carried the story of the missing stained-glass window!

Nancy was amazed. Surely Mr. Bradshaw must have seen the article. Why had he denied knowing about it?

A sudden thought struck the young detective. Bradshaw might be searching for the window himself!

CHAPTER VI

The Paint Clue

NANCY wondered if Mr. Bradshaw knew where the peacock window was.

Suddenly Bess realized that Nancy was not paying attention to the artist. Wondering why, she followed the other girl's gaze and saw the magazine. Instantly she knew Nancy was suspicious. Bess also noticed that Mr. Bradshaw was looking in the young detective's direction.

To warn her friend, Bess said, "Isn't this talk fascinating, Nancy? I had no idea that the art of making stained-glass windows was so intricate."

With a grateful smile at Bess, Nancy nodded and replied, "Yes, it's extremely interesting. But to me, designing the picture would be the most intriguing part."

Mr. Bradshaw's eyes lighted up. "I agree with you a hundred per cent, Miss Drew. And it is probably the most difficult part. Beginners rarely fashion a picture that can be used for a stained-glass window. It takes a great deal of practice to plan a design that will cut into pieces of the right shape."

Presently, not wanting to take any more of Mr. Bradshaw's time, the girls told him how much they appreciated his courtesy and help and said good-by.

As the girls drove off, Bess mentioned the *Continental* and asked Nancy if she thought Mr. Bradshaw knew more than he was willing to admit.

"Yes, I do."

After hearing about the magazine, George remarked, "Well, I can't blame him for wanting to win the reward himself." Then she asked. "Nancy, did you learn anything that might help *you* find the window?"

"Nothing in particular," her friend answered. "But I have a hunch it's in this area."

"Do you think Mr. Bradshaw knows where it is?" Bess questioned.

"Probably not."

"Then it may still be a race," said George enthusiastically. "And I hope you win!"

At Seven Oaks the girls found Susan in the living room, studying picture pamphlets of various automobiles. She looked up and smiled.

"What do you think?" she said, excited. "Cliff wants me to get a new car."

"You're lucky," Bess commented. "Have you decided what make?"

Susan had not made up her mind and was waiting for the girls' advice. "What kind do you all have?" she asked.

Each of the three girls' families had a different make, but both Bess and George declared that Nancy's convertible was their favorite. "If you get one like hers, you'll love it," Bess added.

Susan stood up and said impulsively, "I'll do it. Come on down to the showroom with me and we'll see what they have."

Within an hour they were back at Seven Oaks, with Susan driving her new convertible. George, who had ridden back with her, stepped from the light-green automobile.

"Hypers, this is a record for buying a car!" she said, laughing.

Nancy and Bess arrived in the station wagon just as Cliff came out to inspect the new purchase. He congratulated his wife on her fine selection, then said to Nancy, "While you stay here you're welcome to use either of our cars. There's only one condition attached."

"What's that?"

"You must solve at least one mystery."

Nancy laughed merrily, then asked Susan and Cliff how plans were coming for Garden Week.

"Everything is about ready," Cliff answered. "But the committee is disappointed that the owner of Cumberland Manor still refuses to open it to the public."

"I'm sorry I didn't have better luck on the first try," said Nancy. "But perhaps I can think of another approach."

As the girls entered the front hall of the house, Nancy noticed that a letter addressed to her was lying on a mahogany table. It was from Hannah Gruen.

Nancy read it and frowned. Mrs. Dondo was trying to make trouble again! The woman had been telling people in River Heights that Nancy had left town to avoid paying the hundred dollars that had been lost in the mail. Suddenly Nancy smiled as she read further.

"But don't worry, Nancy. Your father is taking care of things. He went over to her house and talked to her sternly. Mrs. Dondo actually began to tremble and said she would not say anything more against you."

Nancy told Bess and George what the letter said.

"Well good for your dad!" said Bess. "That woman needs to be put in her place."

George spoke up. "But I'm afraid she won't keep her promise. Nancy, you'd better watch out!"

The girls continued to discuss the unpleasant

woman and her brother. When they joined Susan and Cliff on the patio just before dusk, Nancy asked them if they had ever heard of Alonzo Rugby.

Both of them shook their heads, and Cliff looked in the telephone directory. The name was not listed.

"He's an artist," Nancy explained.

"In that case," Cliff said, "the head of the university art department might help us. I'll call him."

He went inside to phone. When he returned, Cliff reported that Alonzo Rugby was not known to the department head.

"That's strange," Nancy remarked. "We were told that he's a talented artist." She related the story Mrs. Dondo had told about her brother, who was supposed to live in Charlottesville.

Obligingly Cliff telephoned an art dealer in town; then Susan called a woman artist in the area. Neither of them had ever heard of Alonzo Rugby.

"Oh, let's forget him," Bess suggested, "and enjoy this heavenly evening."

Nancy did not reply. She knew she could not forget the man. The young detective had a strong hunch that he had been responsible for the fake telegram to her. His only reason for sending it must have been to keep her out of the area. But why?

"If he's 'good for nothing,' as his brother-in-law says," Nancy thought, "he may be involved in some underhanded scheme. But where do I fit in?"

Just then, melodic chimes sounded from inside the house. Anna always rang to announce dinner. The group rose and went inside.

The colonial dining room of Seven Oaks was charming. A crystal chandelier highlighted the handsome mahogany furniture, as well as the exquisite silver candelabra and crystal tumblers on the table.

Clifford said grace, then Anna brought in a heavy silver tureen of soup that she set before Susan. Next, she brought in lovely old china soup plates. She passed them, one by one, after Susan had served the portions.

When the maid left the room, Susan smiled and whispered to the girls, "I try to make things easier for Anna, but she insists on working and serving everything the old-fashioned way. I must confess, though, that I love it."

Cliff's eyes twinkled. "Anna's a rare person," he said. "She sort of lives in the past, and is very much like her mother, who worked for my mother. She imitates her in everything."

After the soup course, Anna brought in a tray of squabs and remarked to the visitors, "I hope you all like my birds."

The "birds" proved to be delicious, as were the

sweet potatoes, corn pudding, and piping-hot biscuits served with them.

Bess said happily, "Don't anybody remind me I'm on a diet!"

Twenty minutes later Anna removed the dishes and carried in individual servings of strawberry shortcake. She had brought in all but Cliff's and was just returning from the pantry with it, when suddenly she shrieked. The dessert slipped from her hand and fell upside down on the floor.

"Good heavens!" she cried out, wringing her hands.

Those at the table stared at the woman in amazement. Anna pointed toward an open side window. "A man with eyes of the devil was looking in here. He was trying to cast a spell on all of us!"

Everyone jumped up and hurried out to the garden in back of the house. It was too dark to see much, but they could hear running footsteps in the distance.

"I suppose it would be hopeless to try to catch the fellow," Cliff remarked.

Nancy said nothing. She was thinking. Perhaps she could pick up a clue to the man's identity. Returning to the house, she hurried to her room and took a flashlight from her suitcase.

By this time the others had come indoors. Susan was trying to assure Anna, who was on the verge of hysterics, that the man had probably meant no harm.

Nancy, meanwhile, had spotted the man's footprints under the window. They led alongside one of the garden paths. About a hundred feet from the house she saw a small metal tube and picked it up. She read:

BLACK
(oxide of iron)

"An artist dropped this!" she surmised. Instantly she thought of Mark Bradshaw, then to Alonzo Rugby. "I must tell Bess and George!"

Nancy turned to go back. At the same moment something hard hit her squarely between the shoulders. She fell forward and lost consciousness!

CHAPTER VII

Jigsaw in Glass

INSIDE the house Bess, George, and the Carrs were talking excitedly about the man who had peered in the window. When Anna described his face, Susan was sure he was the masked man who had caused her first automobile accident.

"I'll call the police," Cliff said, and went to the phone.

Dessert had been forgotten, but suddenly Anna reminded the diners they had not touched their strawberry shortcake.

"I'll fix another helping for Mr. Cliff right away," she said. "You all go back to the dining room."

It was not until they returned to their places at the table that the group realized Nancy had not joined them.

"That's odd," said George. "I saw her come into the house."

She went to the foot of the stairs and called to

the second floor. There was no answer. Worried, George went up and looked around. Coming down, she remarked, "Nancy must have gone outdoors again to do some sleuthing."

"Oh dear," said Susan, "I hope nothing has happened to her!"

Cliff hurried for a flashlight, and the group went outside. He cast the light around and soon spotted the man's footprints. Figuring that Nancy had trailed him, the others followed the marks and soon found the girl's limp body.

"Oh, Nancy!" Bess cried out, terrified. She fell to her knees beside her stricken friend.

To Bess's relief, Nancy opened her eyes. She blinked in the glare of the flashlight and mumbled. "Where is the—the—paint tube?"

The onlookers glanced at one another. Was Nancy delirious? But a second later her mind cleared and she sat up.

"Something hit me in the back. I fell forward, hit my head, and blacked out," she said, looking around. Pointing to a large stone, she added, "I guess someone threw that at me."

"How awful!" Susan exclaimed. Then she told Nancy of her suspicion that the man was the one who had shoved her car off the road.

"I think he was an artist," Nancy said. She told them about the black paint tube. "He apparently knocked me out to take it away from me without being seen. Anyhow, it's gone."

The Carrs helped Nancy to her feet and they

all went into the house. Nancy was immediately put to bed. Not only the police but the Carrs' physician, whom Susan had summoned, arrived in a few minutes.

Dr. Tillett, solicitous and efficient, examined Nancy and announced that she had no serious injuries. He predicted that her back would feel sore for several days, but it would not be necessary for her to stay in bed.

"Just take it easy tomorrow," he advised.

Nancy did not see the police. Cliff had felt it was not necessary and the officers had agreed. But later, when she was alone with Bess and George, the young sleuth remarked, "The tube of paint was a good clue."

"You suspect that Bradshaw or Rugby dropped it?" George asked.

"Yes, I do."

Nancy said that the next morning she would make a paper model of one or two of the footprints. "Then I'll visit Waverly as soon as I can to see if Bradshaw's shoe fits the print."

"Good idea," said George, "but it won't be easy to do."

"I know," said Nancy, yawning wearily, "but I'm going to try it."

The following morning Bess and George helped her make the paper footprint. Luckily the ground was hard enough to permit this. Because of the Carrs' friendship with Bradshaw, the girls did not tell Susan or Cliff what they had in mind.

At luncheon Susan said, "I have an idea. This afternoon we might visit some of the old estates around here. How would you like to see Thomas Jefferson's and James Monroe's homes?"

"Oh, we'd love it!" Bess replied for all the girls.

"And if we have time," Susan went on, "we'll visit some other interesting old places. As we go along, Nancy, you might inquire about the missing stained-glass window."

Nancy was thrilled to make the trip, and the sightseers set off at once. As they drove along, Susan reminded the others that Thomas Jefferson, the third president of the United States, had served as American minister to France. While there he had become interested in Roman architecture after viewing famous ruins. When he returned to Virginia, he designed his home, Monticello, in that style.

"And he was an inventor, too," Susan remarked.

After leaving the car in the visitors' parking lot, the girls walked up to the stately mansion, which stood on a knoll overlooking the rolling Virginia hills. Finally, turning reluctantly away from the lovely view, they went inside the house. There, they admired the beautifully proportioned rooms and the many inventions and conveniences Jefferson had installed in his home.

One arrangement, in particular, attracted the girls. This was a bed set in a space between two rooms so that Mr. Jefferson could get out on either side, depending on whether he wanted to be in his dressing room or in his study. During the day the bed could be drawn into the ceiling to allow free circulation of air between the two rooms.

"That's for me!" Bess exclaimed. "You'd never get out on the wrong side of the bed."

"Let's go on now to James Monroe's home," Susan suggested. "You'll find it more simple, but the gardens have the most beautiful boxwood you've ever seen."

Back in the car again, they drove up the winding mountain road until they came to Ash Lawn. James Monroe, the fifth president of the United States, had built it here to be near his friend Thomas Jefferson.

Susan told them that Ash Lawn was smaller and more informal. A path lined with beautiful boxwood hedges led up to the door. Inside, a mirror hanging on the opposite wall reflected the path, making it appear extremely long.

After leaving Ash Lawn, Susan took the girls to three other estates. At each one Nancy inquired whether the owner had heard of any medieval stained-glass windows in the area that had a peacock in the design. In each case the answer was no.

"I guess we'll have to give up for today," said Susan, glancing at the car clock. "It's getting late."

The girls agreed and they started home. Susan had driven only two miles when she exclaimed, "Why didn't I think of this before!"

"Think of what?" Nancy asked.

"The Dowds. They live around the next bend. They have a perfectly fascinating home, and Mrs. Dowd knows about everything in the neighborhood. If that window is in any home around the Charlottesville area, she'll know it!"

"Then let's talk to her!" Nancy urged.

Susan turned into the winding driveway of the Dowd place and pulled up in front of an austere, white-painted brick mansion. Fortunately Mrs. Dowd was at home. She greeted Susan effusively.

"And bless you, dear, you've brought some very attractive friends," she said. Susan introduced them.

Mrs. Dowd, fiftyish, was a great talker and the girls did not have a chance to say anything. She expressed her delight at meeting the visitors from River Heights and instantly mentioned two people she knew there. Mrs. Dowd bubbled along in the one-sided conversation until Susan finally interrupted diplomatically.

"Nancy would like to ask you some questions," she requested.

"Yes, dear, go ahead," said Mrs. Dowd. "What is it you want to know?"

Nancy quickly told her, and to the girl's elation Mrs. Dowd said, "Well, I declare! Now maybe I can lead you all right to that reward."

Her eyes glistened. "You know, up in our attic, piled in one corner, are parts of a stained-glass window. It was hanging up once. I admit to being a right lazy individual when it comes to working out puzzles, so I've never tried putting the old thing together."

She rose and invited her guests to follow her to the attic. All the way up to the third floor she kept apologizing about the dust and cobwebs that they would probably find, because it was so difficult to get help these days.

"As for myself," said Mrs. Dowd, "I never go near the place!"

Fortunately, there were bright lights in the attic and a large cleared space in the center. The girls brought the glass sections to this spot and got down on their hands and knees to try figuring out how the pieces would fit to make a picture. Mrs. Dowd became so excited that she helped them.

"This is a jigsaw puzzle on a large scale," George remarked.

"And just about as hard," Bess added.

By the end of an hour a large section of the window had been put together. Though the picture was not complete, it was evident that the stained-glass window did not portray a knight riding a white horse and carrying a shield with a peacock design.

Finally Nancy stood up. "Mrs. Dowd," she said, "you've been a wonderful sport, letting us raid your attic and work on this. Unfortunately, this is not the window we're looking for. Would you like us to put the pieces back where they were?"

"Oh no indeed," said Mrs. Dowd. "I declare I'm going to finish this if it takes me a year! I've always been curious to know what this little old window was. I'll get my husband to help me finish putting the pieces together."

The girls then followed Mrs. Dowd down the stairs. As they said good-by to her, she wished them luck in finding the right window.

The road to Susan's home led directly past the Bradshaw farm. Nancy, who had put the paper model of the footprint in her purse, said, "Susan, if it's not too near dinner time, let's call on Mr. Bradshaw. I'd like to ask him a couple of questions."

"All right." Susan turned in at Waverly, saying, "You know I've been in the Bradshaw home several times, but I've never visited the studio. It will be interesting to see it."

As before, the door stood open and Mr. Bradshaw came to greet his visitors. "Susan!" he cried out in delight. "I'm so glad to see you and your friends."

The callers stepped out of the car and walked into the studio. A man of about forty was standing by the bench under which Nancy had found the copy of *Continental*. He was short, dark, and had very bright small eyes.

Mr. Bradshaw waved toward the stranger and said to his callers, "I'd like to present my new assistant. He has been with me a week. This is Mr. Alonzo Rugby."

CHAPTER VIII

An Angry Suspect

BESS was so startled to hear the name of the man the girls were searching for that she gasped and stepped back. Alonzo Rugby's eyes narrowed suspiciously as he came forward to acknowledge the introduction. Mr. Bradshaw looked at Susan and the girls, waiting for an explanation before giving their names to his assistant.

"I—I'm dreadfully sorry," said Bess, recovering. She giggled. "I've heard Mr. Rugby is a famous artist. I was impressed to think I was actually meeting him."

Mr. Bradshaw raised his eyebrows but did not comment. He introduced the girls to Rugby.

"I'm happy to meet you," the assistant said. "I don't know where you heard about my being a great artist. The person must have me mixed up with Mr. Bradshaw. *He's* a great artist. I'm merely a pupil.

Nancy was pleased that at last she had found Mrs. Dondo's brother. She thought, "The first thing I must do is try to find out if his shoes fit my paper pattern."

Nancy noticed that Rugby had taken off his street shoes and put on soft slippers. If she could only find some way to compare the size and shape of his shoes, as well as those of Mr. Bradshaw's, with her paper patterns!

The young sleuth decided that the best way to accomplish this and to watch both men would be to visit the studio as often as possible. As an idea came to her, she said aloud, "Mr. Bradshaw, I'm terribly intrigued by stained-glass window-making. I was wondering if you would mind giving me a few lessons while I'm visiting my cousin?"

The artist looked surprised and did not reply at once. Alonzo Rugby, however, said bluntly, "Mr. Bradshaw is not only a great artist but a very busy man, Miss Drew."

Nancy was fearful that Mr. Bradshaw, backed by his assistant, might refuse her request.

But Susan Carr came to her rescue. Smiling at Mr. Bradshaw, she coaxed, "Oh, Nancy is not a beginner. She has attended art school."

If Mr. Bradshaw had been wavering in his decision, he was persuaded by this remark. "All right," he said. "I'll be happy to give you a few lessons. Suppose you come tomorrow morning."

Nancy was thrilled. Not only could she learn

something from this very fine artist, but perhaps she could unravel the mystery about Mrs. Dondo's brother.

"If he's as bad as Mr. Dondo says, I'm surprised that Mr. Bradshaw would associate with him," Nancy said to herself. Then a troubling thought struck her. Were the two men in league?

"It doesn't seem possible," she decided. "Mr. Bradshaw is such a gentleman." Aloud she said, "I'll be here by ten o'clock. Thank you so much, Mr. Bradshaw."

The girl detective had come close to the artist. Now she surreptitiously put her own foot near his and glanced down to make some quick mental measurements. It looked as if Mr. Bradshaw could definitely be eliminated as the suspect who had injured her.

Nancy maneuvered to get near Alonzo Rugby's street shoes, which he had placed under the bench. She accomplished this when he walked away. As Nancy slid one foot alongside the pair, her heart leaped. The man would bear further investigation!

While Mr. Bradshaw was showing the group a cartoon on which he was working, Alonzo Rugby took Bess by the arm and led her aside. Out of hearing of the others, he whispered, "I want to give you a warning, miss. Don't let your friend come here to take lessons. Mr. Bradshaw's wife is the jealous type. A couple of times when he's had woman students she made life miserable for them. So you had better keep your friend away from here!"

"How do I know this is true?" Bess asked airily.

Alonzo Rugby said she would have to take his word for it. Before he could add anything, Mr. Bradshaw turned around.

"Better get back to the cutting table, Alonzo," he said pleasantly. "We need that glass for tomorrow morning."

Alonzo immediately returned to his work, and Bess joined the others. A few minutes later Susan and her friends left the studio. As they rode toward Seven Oaks, Nancy asked Bess what she and Alonzo had been talking about.

"Making a date?" George asked flippantly.

Bess blushed and said indignantly, "Of course not! But, Nancy, you mustn't go there and take lessons from Mr. Bradshaw!"

"Why not?" Nancy asked in amazement. Bess repeated Rugby's warning.

At once Susan said, "Why, that's utterly ridiculous. Alicia Bradshaw is one of the loveliest women I know. She most certainly is not jealous and never interferes with his work."

Bess looked uncomfortable and her cousin chided her. "I'm surprised at your falling for such a story," George said.

"Well, I'm glad it happened," said Nancy. "Bess has been a bigger help than you give her credit for, George. This convinces me that Alonzo Rugby doesn't want me around that studio."

"But why?" Susan asked.

Nancy told them of her latest conclusions about the man who had peered in the window. "If he *was* Rugby, I'm going to find out!" she said with determination.

"He's dangerous!" Bess exclaimed. "Oh, Nancy, don't go to the studio."

Susan spoke up. "I think Bess is right. If he's the kind of person you think he is, you'd better cancel your appointment."

Nancy said she did not want to miss this opportunity to ferret out the facts. "I'll be perfectly safe with Mr. Bradshaw there. I promise you that if he leaves the studio for long, I'll come home."

Since it had been a busy day, the girls were glad to retire early. The next morning Nancy took her cousin's car and set off for Waverly, the paper footprint in her purse. Bess and George were going to play golf with Susan.

When Nancy reached the studio, both Mr. Bradshaw and his assistant were there. Rugby barely nodded to her and went on with his work. He was cutting glass at a bench.

"Good morning, Nancy," Mr. Bradshaw said cheerfully. "I've been thinking that the best way for you to start learning the window-making process would be to make a few sketches—any kind you wish. Then I'll tell you whether they would divide up well for leading."

He led Nancy to a drawing board, gave her a smock, paper, and some crayons, then went back to his own work.

Nancy sat, lost in thought for several minutes, then drew a sketch of her dog Togo. She used a background of flowering azaleas and forsythia. Not satisfied with the sketch, she next tried a religious subject. In all she made five before calling Mr. Bradshaw.

"I'm ready," she said.

All this time Nancy had been aware that Alonzo Rugby had been watching her covertly. He continually found excuses to leave his workbench and glance at Nancy's sketches. Several times it seemed as though he wanted to say something but had thought better of it and had gone back to his work.

Mr. Bradshaw now looked at the various pictures she had made. "You do have talent," he said, smiling. "I especially like the picture of the little dog. Is he yours?"

Nancy nodded. Mr. Bradshaw finally remarked that while it would not be impossible to make stained-glass windows from any of the sketches, none of them was exactly right for the best leading process.

"When using human figures," he said, "it is

advisable to show them in an upright position. Or, if they're leaning over, they must be seen in profile. The same applies to animals. Your picture of the dog is very appealing, but with the light coming through a window, his figure would look foreshortened."

Nancy thanked the artist for his constructive comments. "I'll make a few more sketches," she said.

A banjo clock on the studio wall had just chimed eleven-thirty when Nancy finished her next one. She had drawn a peacock, its fan spread wide open. She felt that if Mr. Bradshaw and Rugby saw it, possibly one or the other would show any unusual interest he might have in the Greystone window. On impulse, Nancy had made the peacock the size she thought the bird on the shield might be.

"It's pretty good, even if I say so myself," the young sleuth thought.

As she gazed at it, wondering whether she should call Mr. Bradshaw over, the artist suddenly stood up. He announced that he was going outside to look for a flower of a certain shade of blue to use in a window. "I'll be right back," he said.

Nancy fervently hoped Alonzo would follow. Then she could compare his shoe with the paper pattern.

But she was disappointed. The assistant did get

up, but instead of going out the door, he turned and came directly to Nancy's drawing board.

"How do you like it?" she asked casually.

Alonzo snorted. "Pretty bad," he said. "You ought to be ashamed of yourself, taking up Mr. Bradshaw's time. Anyone can see that you're no artist. Where did you get the idea you were?"

Nancy was stunned for a moment by his sharp criticism. She decided, however, that he was still trying to discourage her from coming to the studio.

Aloud she said, "I'll see what Mr. Bradshaw has to say about it."

Alonzo Rugby's eyes blazed. Before Nancy could stop him, he grabbed the sketch from the drawing board, crumpled it into a tight wad, and threw it forcefully across the room. It landed in the fireplace among ashes and half-burned logs!

CHAPTER IX

Surprise Visitors

"Why, how dare you!" Nancy cried out, realizing her sketch was ruined. "You had no right to do that!"

"Yes, I did," Rugby said defiantly, his eyes snapping. "If you haven't got sense enough to get out of here, then I'm the one to see you do!"

Nancy was angry, but also elated. Rugby's sudden rage had probably been caused by the sight of her peacock drawing.

"It could even mean he thinks I know more than I do about the missing window!" she mused.

Nancy pretended to calm down. "Maybe you're right, Mr. Rugby. Suppose you show me some of your sketches for stained-glass windows." Secretly she hoped they would give her a clue to justify her suspicions.

"Very well," Rugby replied haughtily. "But it won't help you any in making sketches yourself. Either you're born with talent or you're not," he added.

He showed Nancy a portfolio of his drawings, all of which seemed mediocre to her. Apparently Mr. Bradshaw had engaged Rugby to help with the mechanical part of stained-glass windowmaking.

After seeing all of the assistant's pictures, Nancy was disappointed. There were no sketches of knights, horses, shields, or peacocks among them.

"Thank you," said Nancy. "I'll try one more sketch before lunchtime."

As she went back to her drawing board, Mr. Bradshaw returned with several delphiniums of various shades of blue. He held them up for Nancy to see.

"They're gorgeous," she said.

"The window I'm working on," Mr. Bradshaw told her, "will picture a garden of these."

For the next half hour only the ticking of the clock could be heard as the three artists worked assiduously. By that time Nancy had a new sketch finished. It portrayed Susan Carr in her rose garden.

Mr. Bradshaw came over to look at it. He smiled broadly. "Now you've caught on, Nancy. This is excellent," he said. "It has design, character, and good line structure, yet it is simple enough to make a good stained-glass window."

Out of the corner of her eye, Nancy looked at Alonzo Rugby. His face was scarlet, and he was casting angry glances in her direction.

"I'm so glad you like it, Mr. Bradshaw," Nancy said with a lilt in her voice, as if she were saying to Rugby, "See, you don't know what you're talking about."

"The woman in this picture looks like Susan Carr. Is it?" Mr. Bradshaw asked.

"Yes," Nancy replied, and added, "Do you suppose you could help me make a small stained-glass window from this? I'd like to give it to my cousin."

"I think so," the artist replied. "We'll start tomorrow morning. I have to close shop now. I have an appointment in town."

Alonzo Rugby took off his lightweight slippers, tucked them into his coat pocket, and put on his shoes. Nancy sighed. There would be no chance to compare either pair of his shoes with the paper pattern of the footprint in the Carr garden.

They all went out, and Mr. Bradshaw locked the door of the studio. Alonzo Rugby said good-by and strode off toward the road. Instead of staying on the gravel path, he stepped onto a little patch of soft earth bordering the driveway. Rugby left perfect imprints of his shoes!

Nancy smiled with satisfaction. The prints would be a good clue. "I'll come back here after dark," she told herself, "and compare the left footprint with my pattern."

It occurred to Nancy that she had better leave something she could pretend to be searching for, in case anyone should find her there. As she walked toward the car with Mr. Bradshaw, Nancy unobtrusively opened her handbag and took out a compact. When he was not looking, she dropped it into some bushes.

"Good-by until tomorrow," she said to the artist, climbing into the car.

At Seven Oaks, Nancy was eagerly questioned by Susan, Bess, and George as to how she had made out with her sketching and sleuthing. She told them what had happened.

"And tonight I'll go back there—to pick up my compact," she said with a chuckle.

Smiling, Bess said, "You'll have an unexpected escort, Nancy."

"What do you mean?"

Her friends explained that after Nancy had left, Ned Nickerson had telephoned. He was leaving Emerson College with Burt Eddleton and Dave Evans, friends of George and Bess. The three football players were on their way to Charlottesville for an annual collegiate conference.

Nancy was delighted. "That's wonderful! And they're coming out here this evening?"

George nodded. "Susan has invited them to dinner. If you really have to go sleuthing tonight,

Nancy," she added, winking at the others, "I'm
sure Ned won't let you go alone."

"And I wouldn't want him to," said Nancy,
grinning broadly.

At seven o'clock that evening the three boys
arrived in a taxi. Susan, who had never met any
of them, peeked through a window as they came
toward the front door.

"That's Ned in the lead," Nancy told her. Ned
was tall, broad-shouldered, and he had brown eyes
and hair.

Dave Evans, who dated Bess, was behind Ned.
The young man had a rangy build, dark hair, and
flashing green eyes. George's favorite escort, Burt
Eddleton, was blond. He was a little shorter and
heavier than the other two.

The girls ran out the front door to greet the
new arrivals. Ned took Nancy aside for a moment
and whispered in her ear, "Miss me?"

"Sure have," she said, and added facetiously,
"but I've been keeping myself busy with Mark
Bradshaw."

"*Who's he?*" Ned demanded.

Nancy teased him, replying that she would explain later.

The boys followed their dates into the house
and Nancy introduced them to Susan, then to
Cliff, who had just come into the living room.

"Good to meet you all," he said.

At dinner the conversation ranged from football to detective work. After dessert, Ned asked for a complete explanation of the mystery Nancy was trying to solve.

"Mysteries, you mean," George corrected.

The boys were astounded to hear all that had happened. Ned was relieved to learn who Mark Bradshaw was, and asked if there was something he could do that very evening to track down the villain. Nancy told him what she had in mind.

"Perfect," he said. "When do we start?"

"Let's go at about eleven o'clock," Nancy suggested. "The Bradshaws probably will be asleep by then."

Shortly before eleven, she and Ned started out in the convertible. The moon would not rise until late, but the stars were shining brilliantly. Ned parked some distance beyond the Bradshaws' driveway. Then the couple walked quietly on the grass along the driveway.

They passed the house without seeing anyone and went on toward the studio. About three hundred feet from it, Nancy whispered, "I suggest that you wait here, Ned. I'm trying to keep my sleuthing a secret. If Mr. Bradshaw or Alonzo Rugby should notice a strange man's footprints alongside mine, they might question me."

Ned agreed and stopped to wait for her in the shadow of some tall bushes. Nancy tiptoed across the driveway and continued to the studio. The young detective was just about to take her flashlight and paper pattern of the footprint from her bag when she became aware of a figure inside the studio.

At that instant the door opened and a flashlight was directed toward Nancy! Quickly she dodged behind the building and by a fraction of a second avoided detection. She heard the door close and footsteps inside.

For an instant Nancy was tempted to run back and get Ned. Then she realized that the intruder in the studio might leave and she would not be able to find out who he was. Cautiously she moved up to one of the windows.

By the time Nancy reached it, the light inside had been extinguished. For several seconds all was silent and dark. Then the light went on again. Nancy gasped!

Alonzo Rugby!

"What in the world is he doing here at this time of night?" Nancy asked herself.

Suddenly Rugby reached inside the fireplace and withdrew a crumpled paper. It was the sketch of the peacock Nancy had made that morning!

Rugby smoothed out the paper on the floor and studied the drawing.

"Why is he so interested in my sketch?" she mused.

As she watched, Alonzo picked up the drawing and slipped it into his portfolio, which he tucked under his arm, and left the studio. To Nancy's amazement, he turned left and headed toward the woods.

"I'd like to know where he's going," Nancy thought, and she began to follow him.

She crept quietly behind the man. This was not difficult because the path among the trees was fairly smooth and Rugby's flashlight, which he held close to the ground, was powerful enough to light her way. She remained a reasonable distance behind the man, who did not turn once.

Presently the path forked. Rugby took the right-hand turn and in a few minutes reached the bank of Eddy Run. He pulled a canoe from the shadows and shoved it into the water. He laid the portfolio on the bottom of the craft, then picked up a paddle and set off upstream toward Ivy Hall and Cumberland Manor.

"He must live up there somewhere," Nancy told herself as she turned back.

Clicking on her own flashlight, Nancy started back through the woods to look for a clear impression of Rugby's footprints. At the intersection of the two paths she found a deep one. She compared the paper pattern with it.

"It's the same length and width!" she exclaimed.

Nancy knew it would be difficult to identify a suspect from just a shoe size. And there were no distinctive marks on the soles or heels of the shoes Rugby had been wearing. In contrast, the pair worn by the man who had pitched the stone at her had contained a small circle in the heel.

"Just the same, I believe that person was Alonzo Rugby," Nancy concluded. "And I'm going to find out all I can about him to prove either his guilt or his innocence!"

The young sleuth had just made this decision when the stillness was shattered by the loud barking of a dog. Nancy soon realized that it was searching for her.

Worried, she decided to take refuge in a tree. Beaming her light around, she quickly shinned up a medium-sized oak tree. Just as she reached the first limb, a large Doberman pinscher bounded into view. He jumped up angrily, pawing the tree.

"Go home! Shoo!" Nancy commanded, but the dog showed no signs of leaving and growled loudly. "I'm literally treed!" she murmured ruefully.

The dog stopped growling long enough for Nancy to hear approaching footsteps. Someone was running in her direction.

"This beast's owner, no doubt," Nancy decided.

The pinscher, intent on his quarry, apparently was not aware that someone was coming. Nancy flashed her light as a guide. A moment later Ned appeared.

"Look out!" she exclaimed in warning.

At the same moment, the pinscher noticed Ned and lunged at him. But the football player neatly

"Ned, look out!" Nancy exclaimed.

sidestepped the dog, Then, with a grip of steel, he grasped the animal by the collar with one hand. The dog snapped and yelped, trying his best to bite Ned.

"Be careful!" Nancy begged.

Suddenly, above the sounds of the growling dog, came a man's icy command. "Stop that, Prince!" To Ned, he cried out, "And you, ruffian, what are you doing here?"

CHAPTER X

The Haunted House

THE speaker, carrying a flashlight, strode into view. Nancy nearly tumbled from her perch in dismay.

The man was Mark Bradshaw!

His mouth set grimly, he stared at Ned, who still held the dog by the collar. An involuntary gasp from Nancy made the artist look up suddenly into the tree. He blinked, then asked, "What is the meaning of this, Nancy?"

As he spoke, Mr. Bradshaw took the pinscher from Ned. The animal immediately quieted down and crouched at his master's feet.

"Mr. Bradshaw," Nancy began, "I'm dreadfully sorry. Before I explain, let me introduce my friend Ned Nickerson. Ned, this is Mr. Bradshaw, the artist who makes stained-glass windows."

Mr. Bradshaw acknowledged the introduction but did not put out his hand to shake Ned's.

Nancy hurried on with her explanation. "I know we're trespassing on your property," she said. "I dropped a compact near the studio this morning and returned to get it. Your dog came after me and I ran. I couldn't think of anything else to do but climb a tree. Ned was waiting for me some distance back. When I didn't return, he came to look for me."

"That's right," Ned said.

"I'd like to come down," Nancy said. "Will you please hold your dog?"

The artist did not reply. He did speak to the pinscher, though, telling him everything was all right and to be quiet. Nancy slid down the tree and stood before Mr. Bradshaw.

"Ned and I will hurry along now and I'll see you in the morning."

Mr. Bradshaw's harsh expression did not relax. In icy tones he said, "We'll forget the whole incident, Nancy. But I shall be busy for the next few days and unable to give you further lessons."

"Please call me," Nancy urged. The young sleuth berated herself for having been caught. She probably had lost her opportunity to keep an eye on Rugby at the studio.

As she and Ned made their way back toward the driveway, Mr. Bradshaw and the dog followed them. Nancy kept flashing her light as if she were looking for the compact. When they reached the studio, she saw it gleaming in the bush. Nancy pounced upon it eagerly, hoping her action might soften Mr. Bradshaw's attitude. Now, believing that she had told the truth, he might let her resume the lessons. But the man walked with them as far as his home without speaking.

"Nice sociable guy," Ned commented later.

Nancy sighed. "He may have heard that I like to solve mysteries and is wondering why I was spying around his place."

When Nancy and Ned reached the Carr home, they heard music and singing. George was doing a comic impersonation. But she stopped in the middle of it and stared at her chum.

"Nancy! You're a mess! What have you been doing?"

"Climbing a tree," Nancy replied and explained about her predicament.

Instead of sympathizing with Nancy, her friends burst into laughter. Burt struck a pose as if holding a newspaper and began reading an imaginary headline:

NANCY DREW, GREAT DETECTIVE,
Treed By Villainous Hound!

"That's enough teasing," Bess announced. "Let's continue our game of imitating famous people."

Nancy changed her clothes and joined the

group. At one o'clock the visiting boys announced they must say good-by. "We'll see you at Emerson for the Spring Dance."

"We'll be there," the girls chorused.

The following morning, when Nancy was relaxing under a large oak tree and wondering how she might find out more about Alonzo Rugby, the rural delivery mailman drove up in his car. Nancy hurried to meet him at the mailbox.

"Good morning," she said. "I hope there's some mail for me."

"If you're Nancy Drew and you're expecting a letter from River Heights, I've brought it," he announced. When Nancy introduced herself and received the letter, the mailman added, "You know, I deliver a good many letters from River Heights."

Instantly Nancy was on the alert. "You mean to Alonzo Rugby?"

"Yes. You know him? I think the letters are from his sister."

"Oh yes—Mrs. Dondo is a neighbor of mine in River Heights," Nancy remarked.

"Mr Rugby boards at a small farm on Uplands Road," said the friendly mailman. "The place is owned by a widow named Mrs. Paget."

The letter carrier now said good-by and drove off. Nancy stood lost in thought. She had driven along Uplands Road the previous day. Not only was it nowhere near Eddy Run, but Mrs. Paget's farm was in the opposite direction from that which Rugby had taken in the canoe the evening before.

"Where was he going at that hour?" Nancy mused. "Maybe I can find out from Mrs. Paget!"

Nancy opened a letter from her father and learned that Mrs. Dondo had stopped gossiping to the neighbors about her. But she insisted upon prosecuting Mr. Ritter to get her hundred dollars. Mr. Drew stated that if his daughter could unearth any clues in Charlottesville, it would help a great deal.

Hurrying to the house, Nancy delivered several letters to the others. Then she told them what her father had written and how she had learned where Rugby lived.

"I'm going over there at the first opportunity," she said.

Nancy knew it would not be possible to go that day because Susan was having a party in the girls' honor that evening and needed her car for several errands. Cliff had already left in his.

"We ought to help with the party, anyway," Nancy said to Bess and George.

At luncheon, Cliff made an announcement. "You girls have turned me into a detective. Nancy, do you remember telling me you were going to see if any Greystones ever lived in this area? Well, I found out for you."

"Oh, thank you, Cliff. What's the answer?"

"I contacted a historical authority of this area. He said there weren't any Greystones around the Charlottesville area in eighteen fifty. So I'm afraid, you're not going to find your stained-glass window here, Nancy," Cliff deduced.

Nancy laughed. "I'm not giving up yet!"

The Carrs' guests were to arrive about seven o'clock that evening. Nancy was the first of the three girls to finish dressing. After a final glance in the mirror, she left her room to go downstairs. Passing Susan and Cliff's bedroom she overheard Susan say, "Alicia Bradshaw phoned and said that she and Mark would not be able to come tonight. She gave no reason. Do you suppose it could be because of what happened last night to Nancy?"

Cliff said something in a low voice and Nancy went on downstairs. The last thing she wanted to do was cause any difficulty between Susan and her friends! For a moment she even toyed with the idea of going home, but thought better of it immediately.

"If the Bradshaws are staying away because of me, I think they're acting very strangely."

Nancy forgot the episode when the Carrs, Bess, and George joined her a few minutes later. Soon the guests began to arrive. The girls from River Heights found them all delightful people.

Before long, a good-looking young man named Paul Staunton sought out Nancy. When supper was announced, he asked if he might serve her from the buffet table.

Paul's hope of talking to Nancy alone as they carried their plates out onto the patio was shattered.

"Oh, good night," he said, as they noticed a woman approaching. "Here comes that actress, Sheila Patterson. She'll take over the conversation!"

Nancy smiled. When she had met the forty-year-old widow earlier, the girl had found her effusive. The attractive woman had insisted at once that Nancy call her by her first name. Sheila had said she was completely worn out. She was not in a play at the moment but resting at Ivy Hall, an estate she had recently purchased. Nancy recalled it as the overgrown place she had seen not far from Bradshaw's.

Now, reaching Nancy and Paul, Sheila said dramatically, "Nancy, darling, I've just learned that you're simply marvelous at solving mysteries. I have a devastating one for you."

Nancy's eyes widened. "What is it, Sheila?"

Of medium height and slender build, Sheila had coal-black hair with a dramatic white streak in the front. Her face was youthful, with winged eyebrows that gave her an inquisitive look.

"It's about Ivy Hall," the actress replied. "I adored the place at first, but now it has become horribly spooky. My daughter Annette and I hear ghostly footsteps at night and a peacock has appeared on our lawn several times."

"A peacock!" Paul laughed, but Nancy tensed.

Sheila stopped speaking and shuddered. She leaned close to Nancy and in a strange, tremulous voice said, "Nancy, do you know what bad luck a peacock can bring a person?"

CHAPTER XI

Cowboy Luke

STRANGE noises . . . ghostly footsteps . . . peacocks! At once Nancy was intrigued by Ivy Hall.

Recalling that Sheila Patterson had just asked her a question, Nancy answered, "All I've ever heard is that it is unlucky to wear a peacock feather."

"Let me tell you!" Sheila cried out dramatically. "They bring bad luck—disaster!" The woman buried her face in her hands. "That peacock on my lawn! I know what it means. I'll never get another part in a play!"

Although she believed the woman was exaggerating her fear, Nancy felt genuinely sorry for her. She had often met persons who had let superstitions affect their lives, but Nancy was astounded that a person of Sheila's talent and intelligence could believe such an absurd thing.

Taking the actress's hand, Nancy asked her to sit down and talk it over.

Paul Staunton had been standing all this time. Now he said, "Perhaps you two would like to be alone. I'll be back later, Nancy."

The young sleuth flashed an appreciative smile, then turned to Sheila. "Please try not to be upset about the mystery at your home. You know, most people believe peacocks bring good luck, not bad luck."

"No, I never heard that," Sheila answered absently, calming down a bit. But she started to twist a lace handkerchief nervously. Looking pleadingly into Nancy's eyes, she said, "It would give me a lot of hope and confidence if you'd come to Ivy Hall for a few days. Maybe I'm foolish, but until I find out there's nothing supernatural going on, I must believe that there's only bad luck in store for me."

"I'd like to come," said Nancy thoughtfully, "but——"

"Yes?"

Nancy said she had come south with her friends Bess and George. If she went to Ivy Hall, she would want them to accompany her. Also, since they were Susan's guests, she must first speak to her cousin.

"Oh, I intended to ask your two friends to come," Sheila said warmly, "and I know Susan won't mind." She hugged Nancy and gave her a light kiss on the cheek. "You're a darling—a perfect darling! Come tomorrow. I can't stand it much longer with just Annette and me there. I'd move out, but I've put all my money into the place. The whole thing is dreadful! My nerves are nearly shattered!"

At that moment Sheila's daughter, Annette, came up and put her arm around her mother's shoulders. The girl appeared to be about eighteen years old, had beautiful curly auburn hair, and a turned-up nose. Small-boned, she walked and moved in a quick, elfinlike manner.

After speaking to Nancy, she said, "Mother, dear, perhaps we'd better go. You're becoming too excited."

"Oh, I'm all right now," Sheila said, looking at her daughter affectionately. "And what do you think, my love? Nancy Drew and her friends are coming to stay with us and solve our mystery!"

"We'll try, anyway," Nancy said, smiling.

Annette Patterson looked relieved. "Well, I'm glad to hear that. Thanks a million. But I must say, Nancy, you have courage!"

Nancy told the Pattersons that if Susan had not made plans for them for the next two days, she, Bess, and George would be at Ivy Hall in the morning.

"Thanks, darling." Sheila hugged Nancy.

As soon as the actress and her daughter left, Paul Staunton returned with fresh plates of food, and he and Nancy spent the rest of the evening together. After all the guests had left, the Carrs sat down with their visitors for a chat.

"The party was super," said George.

"Dreamy," was Bess's comment.

Nancy mentioned what a delightful time she had had, also how much she had enjoyed the Carrs' friends.

"And they all like you girls," Susan said. With a chuckle she glanced at Nancy and added, "Particularly Paul Staunton."

Nancy blushed. "He's a lot of fun."

"I noticed," said Cliff, "that Sheila had you cornered. What was all the conversation about?"

Nancy told the group of Sheila's invitation, then asked Susan if she would mind their accepting.

"Go ahead, by all means. But don't forget Garden Week. We have some dates then, you know."

Cliff spoke. "How about Cumberland Manor, Nancy? Have you given up trying to persuade Mr. Honsho to open it for us?"

"No. As a matter of fact, it's because there may be a peacock in each place that I'm going to Ivy Hall. Maybe, just maybe, there's a connection!"

"That's right," Cliff agreed. "Nancy, you amaze me."

Susan offered the use of her car, telling Nancy to keep it as long as she wished.

Bess sighed. "I was almost hoping you'd object," she said. "Ugh! Ghosts and peacocks!"

The three girls packed their suitcases before going to bed and were up early the next morning. At ten o'clock, after one of Anna's special breakfasts, they set off for Ivy Hall. On reaching the entrance to the untended, overgrown grounds, Nancy turned in and drove up to the colonial red-brick house, the sides of which were thickly covered with ivy. It had an impressive front porch with majestic white columns.

On the steps stood Annette Patterson and a young man. The girl, who was shaking her head vigorously, looked annoyed.

"Well, what do you know!" Bess exclaimed. "That's the same 'cowboy' we saw at Cumberland Manor—the one who wouldn't talk to us!"

Just then the young man jumped on his bicycle and pedaled quickly past them and down the driveway.

"We'll ask Annette about him later," Nancy remarked, as the girls alighted from the car.

Annette, who was wearing pink shorts and a candy-striped blouse, ran toward the girls with a happy "Hi!" Then, Sheila, similarly attired, hurried from the hall. Being more effusive than her daughter, she planted resounding kisses on the cheeks of her visitors.

"You are lambs to come!" Sheila cried gaily, hooking one arm into Nancy's and leading the girls into the house. "Isn't this a heavenly place?" she asked.

"Yes, it's charming," replied Nancy, admiring the large center hall with its graceful, wide stairway.

"Let's take the girls on a tour of inspection, Mother," Annette said enthusiastically.

Sheila led the way first into the living room to the left of the hallway, then the dining room on the right. They were sunny and spacious, but draperies and wallpaper were faded and in places badly worn. The chairs and tables were in need of repair.

"I bought the house furnished," Sheila said, "and intend to renovate when I can. But for now——" She shrugged, then went on. "Annette and I always lived in hotels until recently."

"But never again, I hope!" Annette said fervently. "I love Ivy Hall and never want to leave it."

"Unless we're forced to," her mother said sadly.

"I'm sure it won't come to that," Nancy said.

French doors at the end of the living room led to a walnut-paneled library, practically bare of furniture. Bess glanced at its bookless shelves and shuddered inwardly. The room, a dark one, was eerie looking.

Sheila hurried her guests out of it, led them

through a modern pantry and kitchen, then out onto a screened porch off the dining room. Here, she said, they spent a great deal of time in mild weather.

"I would, too," Nancy commented, glancing at the comfortable lounge chairs.

Annette pointed out the old slave quarters, a hundred and fifty feet away, now tumble-down and covered with ivy. "That's where all the cooking was done in the old days," she explained.

"How interesting!" Bess murmured.

Sheila sighed. "The gardens are dreadful, but we have no help. I put every cent we could spare into buying the place, and the upkeep——" She stopped speaking. Apparently a thought she did not want to put into words had come to her.

"Mother and I are sort of camping out here," Annette said in her direct way. "Even if we could afford it, I doubt that we could find servants willing to come here. We had one and she spread talk of the house being haunted." Then she added with a smile, "I hope you girls don't mind having simple meals."

"Oh, we'll be glad to help," Bess offered.

George laughed. "If you make Bess chief cook, you can be sure of always having a real feast."

Next, Sheila and Annette showed the girls the rambling second floor of Ivy Hall, with its six bedrooms and two baths. Undoubtedly it, too, had once been very beautiful, but now it needed redecorating. The mahogany woodwork was scarred and the long hall carpet threadbare.

"This will be your bedroom," Sheila told the girls, throwing open a paneled door. "It overlooks the old slave quarters."

The room was large, its windows adorned with faded but lovely damask draperies. A huge canopied bed and a cot with a flowered quilt stood along one wall. The other furniture was simple.

After lunch Nancy, Bess, and George unpacked. They spent the rest of the day with Annette, wandering around the estate. Nancy was particularly interested in a closed stairway at the end of the second-floor hall. It led to the attic.

"It may come in handy to know about this," she said half-jokingly, winking at George.

By suppertime the girls had thoroughly memorized the layout of the house and the grounds.

"I could almost find my way around in the dark," Nancy said, but Sheila assured her that this would not be necessary. There were electric lights everywhere except the attic.

When the visitors said good night at ten o'clock and went upstairs, Annette followed them into their room and sat down to chat. She asked about River Heights and the girls' friends. Nancy described their home town briefly, and Bess spoke enthusiastically of Ned, Burt, and Dave. Then Nancy mentioned the young man she had seen on the Pattersons' porch that morning.

"Is he someone you date?" she asked Annette.

The girl looked blank for a moment. Then she said, "Oh, you mean Luke Seeny."

Bess giggled. "Is he a real cowboy?"

"Yes, he is—from Oklahoma. I met him at a dance. Luke's been trying to date me for over a week, but I don't care for him. All he does is brag about his wealthy family back home."

"Where does he stay here?" Nancy inquired.

"At a hotel in Charlottesville."

This information surprised Nancy and her friends, who had expected to hear that Luke lived with Mr. Honsho at Cumberland Manor.

"What is Luke doing in Charlottesville?" George asked.

"Oh, nothing special, I guess," Annette answered. "Just sightseeing."

The other girls exchanged glances. Luke's story about doing nothing in particular did not ring true, but they did not mention this to Annette. Presently she rose, said good night, and wished them pleasant dreams.

"I wish so, too," said Bess, after Annette had closed the door. "Ivy Hall gives me a funny feeling. It's hard to describe, but even if I hadn't heard that the place is haunted, I'd have thought so myself."

"Now, Bess," Nancy said with a grin, "you don't mean that!"

George gave her cousin a look of reproach.

"You'll sleep sounder than any of us," she prophesied, "and in the morning you'll take back those words."

Bess and George climbed into the canopied bed, since Nancy insisted that she would sleep on the cot. With the lights out, Ivy Hall seemed extremely dark and quiet. There was not a sound in the house, and outside only the chirping of crickets could be heard. Soon all three girls were sound asleep.

About midnight Nancy was awakened by sounds of someone moving around in the attic. Listening intently, she could distinctly hear boards creaking overhead.

Bess and George awoke too. There was no doubt that someone was walking in the attic.

"The ghost!" Bess shrieked.

CHAPTER XII

A Weird Disappearance

"OH, it's true!" Bess cried out. "There *are* ghosts in this house." She dived under the covers and lay motionless.

George turned on the night-table lamp and said, "Shame on you, Bess. We came here to help Nancy solve the mystery. Get up! Let's go!"

"You—you tell me about it later," Bess said unhappily.

Nancy was already up and putting on her robe and slippers. George donned her own, then put Bess's slippers on her.

As Nancy turned the doorknob she said quietly, "Never mind, George. The two of us can go."

"Oh, I don't want to be left alone!" Bess cried out. "Wait for me!" She quickly put on her robe and followed Nancy and her cousin into the hall.

Annette, in pajamas, was standing outside her

own bedroom, a look of fright on her face. "You heard it, too?" she whispered.

In a low voice Nancy said, "We're going up to the attic. Want to come?"

"Oh, you'd better not! Something might happen to you," Annette warned. "I wouldn't dare go, anyway. I promised Mother I never would."

Nancy quietly opened the door to the attic stairway. She looked on the wall for a light switch, then remembered there was none.

"You'll have to use a candle," Annette said.

On a small table in the hallway stood a glass candleholder with a short white candle in it. Annette picked up a packet of matches beside it and with trembling fingers lighted the candle. Nancy, meanwhile, chided herself for leaving her flashlight in the car.

"Here you are," Annette said, handing the candle to Nancy, who went at once to the stairway.

The creaking sounds above had not been repeated. Bess, last in line, said in a shaky voice, "The ghost must be hiding!"

The others did not comment. Reaching the top step they looked around cautiously. Several old curved-top trunks stood about, discarded draperies hung on lines, and large paintings in ornate gold frames were propped against the eaves.

Nancy set the candle down on a table in the

middle of the room and the three girls began looking behind various objects to see if anyone were
hiding. They found no one. Next, Nancy started
to open trunks to determine if the "ghost" were
inside. As she lifted back the lid of the third one,
Bess gasped and Nancy and George stepped back
in horror.

A little girl, her eyes closed, lay in the trunk!

For a moment the three stared, horrified. Then
suddenly they smiled. The figure was that of a
very large lifelike doll! The rest of the trunks
were examined but revealed no one hiding inside.

As Nancy and George stood gazing about the
attic, wondering if there were any other entrance,
Bess became fascinated by a large painting at one
end of the room. The picture portrayed a dashing
cavalier, his waxed mustache perfectly groomed.
The man's turned-up hat was worn at a rakish
angle, with a feather curled smartly over his
shoulder.

The cavalier's eyes seemed to stare at Bess as she
walked about. Drawn to it like a magnet, she went
to the far side of the attic to examine the gallant
gentleman's face. It looked so real that it seemed
almost to be alive.

Nancy and George, meanwhile, had been studying the wall on the opposite side of the attic. It
was higher than any of the other three unfinished
walls and was paneled. The two girls walked

toward it to see if there might be a concealed entrance to another room.

Hearing a slight gasp, Bess turned around. To her astonishment, neither of the other girls was in sight.

"Nancy! George! Where are you?" she called.

Bess's heart began to pound. Her friends must have gone downstairs without her!

"I'm not going to stay up here alone," she told herself, and headed for the stairway.

As Bess picked up the candle, she stopped short in panic. A few feet ahead of her stood a swaying form in white. *The ghost!*

Bess stared at it, too terrified to utter a sound. Suddenly the figure took a step toward her. With a great leap Bess passed it, dashed toward the stairway, and raced down the steps pell-mell, making a terrific clatter.

Annette, hearing her, hurried to the foot of the stairs. One look at Bess's terrified expression convinced her that the girl must have seen something frightening in the attic.

"What was it?" she cried out, taking the candle from Bess's trembling hand.

"A—a—gh-ghost!" Bess wailed and slumped to the floor. Her legs would no longer hold her.

"Then it's true! The house is haunted!" Annette cried out.

Bess nodded and in a frantic whisper asked, "Where are Nancy and George?"

"What do you mean?" Annette asked. "Weren't they with you?"

Bess stared in stupefaction. "You—you mean they didn't come d-down here?"

"No."

Bess gave a cry of alarm. "Then they're gone!" she moaned. "The ghost got them!"

The commotion had awakened Sheila Patterson. Now she hurried into the hall in a frilly nightgown. On hearing what had happened, she paced back and forth, waving her arms dramatically and crying out, "Oh, what will we do? What will we do?"

"We could call the police," said Annette.

Bess, though frightened, realized that if Nancy and George were in trouble, she must help them at once. They could not wait for the police!

Bess's courage returned. She stood up and said with determination, "Come on, Annette! We'll have to go back to the attic and rescue Nancy and George!"

Sheila grabbed her daughter's arm. "No, you mustn't go! I won't let you!"

"Mother, we have to do *something!*" Annette urged. "Nancy and George were willing to come here and risk their lives to help us. It's our responsibility if something has happened to them!"

"Oh, I know—I know!" moaned Sheila.

A thought came to Bess. "You know, my cousin sometimes plays tricks on me," she spoke up.

"Maybe George found a sheet in the attic and played ghost to scare me!"

Somewhat reassured, Sheila finally agreed to allow her daughter to go up to the attic. As Bess started up the steps, the actress's conscience began to bother her.

"I'm going along," she said.

Bess reached the top and held the candle high. As she paused to look around, a current of air suddenly blew out her light.

Standing almost paralyzed in total darkness, she heard a door somewhere in the old house squeak eerily, then close with a terrific bang!

Ten minutes earlier, Nancy and George had been walking across the attic toward the panel wall. Without warning, the floor had opened beneath their feet!

The girls found themselves shooting down a steep wooden slide into pitch blackness. A trap door above them closed quietly. They landed abruptly on a hard surface at the bottom of the chute.

"Oh, my head!" George groaned. "Nancy, are you all right?"

"I guess so. I banged my shoulder a little."

The two friends untangled themselves and slowly stood up. Both groped around and could feel with the tips of their fingers a dank ceiling a few inches above their heads.

"Where do you suppose we are?" George asked.

"In the cellar, probably." Nancy smiled. "That was a fast ride!"

George sighed. "Where do we go now?"

Nancy ran her fingers over the slippery surface of the slide. "We never could crawl up that long chute," Nancy replied. "We'll have to try getting out of here some other way."

The girls stood still a few minutes, waiting to see if Bess would also shoot down the slide. They braced themselves to catch her. Nancy called up the opening, telling Bess what had happened.

"Turn on the light in the cellar and open the door, will you?" she shouted.

There was no answer. "I suppose," said George, "that when Bess missed us, she got out of the attic in a hurry."

"No doubt. George, what I can't understand is why the trap door opened all of a sudden. I'm sure we walked over it several times before."

George whispered in Nancy's ear, "There's only one answer. That ghost we were trying to find must have opened it."

"Which means," Nancy replied in a low tone, "that he may still be at the top of this slide in a niche. Well, George, we'll have to rescue ourselves. Let's start."

Nancy ran her hands along the ceiling, floor, and side walls. "I think we must be in some kind of a tunnel. Maybe it was an old one used by the slaves years ago and led from their quarters to the main house."

"Well, the sooner we get to the end of it, the happier I'll be," George replied. "Let's go!"

The girls got down on their hands and knees and began to inch their way along the floor, side by side. They felt ahead cautiously before moving forward.

After progressing some twenty-five feet, George said, "This sure is slow work." Her knees began to burn and she was sure most of the skin had been scraped off them.

Fifty feet beyond, the two came to a heavy door and stood up to examine it. The door had a huge, old-fashioned iron latch and slide bolt, both of which were coated with rust. Though the girls pushed with all their strength to move them, Nancy and George were not able to budge the bolt even a fraction of an inch.

"Dead end!" George remarked woefully.

"I'm afraid so," Nancy answered. "We'll have to go back where we started from and try the other direction."

This time the girls felt it was safe to walk upright. With Nancy on the right and George on the left, they moved fairly rapidly, but each kept one hand on the wall nearest her. By the time they reached the spot where Nancy thought they would find the slide, George was considerably in the lead.

"Wait!" Nancy called. She was going to say that from this point on they should crawl when George cried out from the pitch blackness, "Help!"

"What's the matter?" Nancy asked quickly.

There was no response and suddenly Nancy could hear the splash of water. George must have fallen into a well or pit!

CHAPTER XIII

The Slave Tunnel

NANCY dropped to her knees and crawled forward rapidly. In a moment she reached what seemed to be a pool.

"George, where are you? Answer me!" she cried, fear gripping her.

Then, to her intense relief, George replied, "I'm all right but I went down under water. Keep talking, so I can swim toward your voice."

Nancy encouraged George, who said the water was icy cold. A few seconds later the two girls touched hands and Nancy pulled her friend out of the underground water hole.

"Thank goodness you're all right!" Nancy exclaimed. "I wonder how wide the pit is." She feared that escape this way was cut off.

George said the pit seemed very large to her, but perhaps she was overestimating its size.

"I'll try to find out," said Nancy.

While Nancy felt her way along the edge of the water, George remained behind, trying to wring out her soaking-wet bathrobe and pajamas. She had lost her slippers in the water.

"This appears to be more like a large well," Nancy surmised. "It's only in the center of the tunnel. I think we can creep along the edge safely and get to the other side of the water."

George crawled after Nancy. Foot by foot, they went on without coming to the end of the tunnel.

"This must run all the way to Charlottesville," said George disgustedly.

Nancy was growing more concerned about their predicament. Suppose this end of the tunnel was blocked also!

To keep up George's spirits as well as her own, Nancy said with a chuckle, "If the slaves had to walk along this bumpy path carrying trays of food, they must have had a lot of spills."

"I'll say," George replied. "Can't you just see a big silver tray with a freshly roasted turkey being dropped upside down on this earthen floor!"

The remark made both girls laugh, and each felt better. Suddenly Nancy's outstretched hand touched a wooden step.

"End of the trail!" she said happily as the two friends inched their way up the stairs.

The flight was very steep, and at the top Nancy could not feel any doorknob, latch, or lock.

George had no better luck. "The exit has been

boarded up!" she said fearfully. "What do we do now?"

Nancy did not reply. She began to look for a way to slide or rotate a section of the wall. Suddenly, her fingertips caught on a narrow crevice and the end of a panel moved slightly.

"It's a sliding door," Nancy reported. "Help push!"

Together, the two girls stuck their fingers into the tiny opening and shoved. The panel began to give, but it squeaked and groaned loudly.

"Spooky!" George remarked, as the girls squeezed through the narrow opening.

Nancy and George found themselves in a large closet filled with dishes. At the opposite side was a door with a handle, which opened easily.

The friends walked into the kitchen of Ivy Hall. Moonlight streamed through the windows. It was a welcome relief from the total darkness of the tunnel.

"Thank goodness we're freed!" George exclaimed.

The closet door swung shut with a tremendous bang, which made both Nancy and George jump.

"The noise probably scared the Pattersons and Bess out of a year's growth!" George said, as they walked toward the front hall.

The girls ascended the stairs and Nancy called, "Bess! Annette! Sheila!"

Instantly footsteps came pounding down the

attic steps. In a few moments the group had assembled in the second-floor hall.

"Nancy! George!" Bess cried out. "Where have you been? We thought the ghost got you!"

"Not us," her cousin retorted.

Bess pointed. "Look at you!"

Nancy and George glanced down and saw that their pajamas and robes were streaked with dirt.

"George, you're soaking wet!" Annette cried out.

George laughed. "I've been swimming."

"What happened to you girls?" Sheila asked.

Nancy and George described their harrowing experience.

"I didn't know about the trap door and the tunnel," Sheila said, shivering a little.

When Nancy heard that Bess had really seen a ghost, her eyes opened wide. This meant that the impersonator could not have been hiding below the trap door after she and George went through it.

Nancy looked at Bess questioningly. "Did that ghost come down the attic stairs?"

"No."

"Well, he didn't follow George and me," she said. "That means he must still be in the house. We're going to find him!"

Sheila Patterson stared in amazement. "How can you find a ghost? It's not real!"

Nancy said she was certain that Bess's ghost

was a human being. "And I intend to locate him! Come on, everybody!" she urged.

With Nancy in the lead, holding the candle, the entire group trooped to the attic. Bess almost expected to see the ghost standing near the stairway, but there was no sign of it. The attic was apparently deserted.

"If the ghost is a real person, he might be hidden!" Bess said nervously.

"We'll smoke him out!" George said with determination. "But, for goodness sake, don't anybody step on the trap door!"

Nancy held a candle close to the floor, which made the trap plainly visible. She got down alongside it and pushed on the door. It would not open!

"That's strange," she remarked. "This trap door must work by some mechanism we aren't aware of."

The girl detective moved to the paneled wall, which had aroused her curiosity earlier. Now she examined every inch of it. Suddenly she cried out, "I think I've found the secret!"

The others crowded around as she silently slid back the whole section of panel. No one was hiding in the small enclosure beyond.

"This is probably where your ghost came from, Bess," Nancy judged.

"Sure," George agreed. "And the ghost used a sheet from that open trunk full of linen."

"Where have you been?" Bess cried. "We thought
the ghost got you."

Nancy handed the candle to George. "Hold this and shine the light in here, will you?"

George did this while Nancy tested the flooring behind the panel. Finding it firm, she stepped inside. On the front wall she found a lever and pushed it.

The trap door opened downward!

"Oh!" cried Bess, blinking rapidly.

Annette announced, "Nancy, you're a genius!"

George was thoughtful. "I can't understand what the slide is doing there and who put it in."

Nancy thought it might have been used to transfer supplies from the attic to the tunnel. "Perhaps during the Civil War," she added, "Ivy Hall's owner installed it."

After Nancy closed the trap door and pulled the panel shut, she suggested that they all go downstairs and get some sleep.

"I don't feel like closing my eyes while that masquerader is still around," Bess protested.

"Nor I," Annette admitted.

When they reached the second floor, Nancy put an arm around Bess. "I think the ghost followed you down the attic steps. While you were talking to Sheila and Annette, he probably slipped into the bedroom at the end of the hall, then escaped when the three of you returned to the attic."

"Things have gone too far around here!" Sheila cried out, excited. "Girls, we're not staying here another minute. I want everyone to pack immediately."

The others were shocked by the actress's order. Annette spoke up quickly. "But, Mother, it's the middle of the night. By the time we pack and get ready to leave, it will be dawn, anyway."

"I don't care *what* time it is!" Sheila burst out, her eyes flashing. "I won't live in a house with a ghost—spook or human—another minute!"

Annette looked unhappy. "I don't blame you, Mother, but if we stick it out, we may find the explanation. Besides, it's our home."

"Suppose two of us stand guard while the others sleep," George suggested.

Sheila finally said reluctantly, "All right, we'll see what happens."

Nancy and Bess went on the first two-hour watch, sitting in chairs near the attic entrance. Then George and Annette took over. Morning dawned without anything having happened.

After a few hours of unbroken rest, Sheila actually began to sing. With the girls' help she prepared a delicious breakfast and they all sat down on the porch to eat.

"I'm sorry I became so hysterical last night," she said contritely. "I've been thinking things over calmly, but it still seems to me that it would be foolish for any of us to stay here."

Nancy said, "I believe that is what the ghost is hoping you'll think."

"What do you mean?" the actress asked, puzzled.

"He believes something valuable is hidden here and is looking for it," Nancy continued. "He must be familiar with the place, since he knows about the trap door. Sheila, if you leave, the ghost will have the run of the place. You own this property and anything hidden on it is yours. You might be cheating yourself out of some valuable object if you move away."

"I suppose so," the actress conceded. "Do you think Ivy Hall's treasure might be money?"

"I doubt it," said Nancy. "But I do have one theory regarding what the treasure might be."

She told the Pattersons about the missing stained-glass window and the reward being offered for its recovery. "That's the real reason why Bess, George, and I came to Virginia."

"How simply fascinating!" Annette exclaimed.

Nancy asked Sheila if any former owner of the place was named Greystone. The actress could not recall whether any of the old deeds showed that a family by that name had ever lived there.

"Before I purchased Ivy Hall, Annette and I looked at the property carefully. We saw nothing to indicate that a stained-glass window was ever built into any of the walls," the actress said.

Nancy was thoughtful. Her mind was busy trying to determine who might be playing ghost. "The one most likely," she decided, "is Alonzo

Rugby." Aloud she said, "The window may have been taken out and put somewhere. Anyway, why don't we all hunt for a clue to it?"

"Yes, let's!" Annette urged.

Walls, floors, cabinets, and closets were investigated but yielded no clue.

"If the window was removed," George said, "then it may have been taken apart and the pieces packed away. So I'd say it's back to the attic for us!"

Every trunk and box in the third floor was emptied. The girls were fascinated by the old costumes—the accumulation of several generations of Ivy Hall inhabitants. But no real treasure came to light and no stained glass was found.

"Nancy, I'm sure there's nothing of much value around here," said Sheila.

"Unless the ghost found it last night and took it with him," Bess suggested.

Nancy smiled. "In that case," she said, "he won't be back."

This reasoning made Sheila change her mind about moving out at once. She agreed to stay one more night at least.

Nancy was pleased to hear this and reminded her that they had not examined the tunnel or the slave quarters.

"I can't!" Sheila exclaimed. "I'm exhausted. You girls do it."

Nancy took her flashlight and a wrench from

the car, and led the way through the secret door of the dish closet.

When the girls reached the pool into which George had fallen, she laughed. "Probably this was where the slaves paused to fill pitchers on their way to serve meals."

Nancy stopped at the slide and looked up. Wooden boards had been nailed over a stairway to convert it to a chute. Soon the searchers reached the end of the tunnel.

Using the wrench, Nancy hammered back the rusted bolt. The door creaked open and the girls walked into the remains of a kitchen.

"The slave quarters!" Annette exclaimed.

Part of the building had caved in. In the rubble Nancy saw an ornamental sheet of cast iron. Walkover to it, she threw the light directly on the design. The others crowded around.

"A peacock!" Bess cried out. "Where was this used?"

Annette explained that it was a fireback, set in the rear of a fireplace to reflect heat into the room. It had probably been used many years ago in one of the rooms of Ivy Hall.

"Now I'm convinced," said Nancy, "that residents of this house were interested in peacocks as a design."

"Yes," said Bess, "but it doesn't prove that the stained-glass window was ever here."

Nancy did not comment, but as she started

back through the tunnel, she said, "I'll look outdoors for footprints of the ghost."

Leaving the others in the kitchen, she went down the back-porch steps and began a systematic search for prints. Suddenly she saw something that made her gasp in amazement.

At the top of her voice, Nancy cried out, "Come here, everybody!"

CHAPTER XIV

A Midnight Chase

IMMEDIATELY the Pattersons hurried to Nancy's side, followed by Bess and George. The young sleuth was down on hands and knees outside a basement window that was almost completely hidden by a heavy growth of shrubbery.

"Careful where you walk!" she called out. "Here are some peculiar footprints."

The others followed Nancy's pointing finger. Deeply embedded in the sod and dirt were the prints of a three-toed bird.

Sheila looked alarmed. In a trembling voice she asked, "Do they belong to a peacock?"

"Yes and no," Nancy replied ambiguously.

The others waited for her to explain. After making some measurements, she looked up and said, "See these marks. Sometimes they're close together, and at other times far apart."

"What does that prove?" Bess asked.

"It means," said Nancy, "that a human being and not a bird made these marks."

Annette paled. "You—you mean a human being with a bird's feet?" she questioned.

Nancy said that she believed the human being had strapped artificial peacock claws to the bottom of his shoes to avoid making footprints that might be recognizable.

Bess asked her if she had any theory about who the intruder had been.

"Yes," Nancy replied. "I think it was our ghost friend. And he's more interested in peacocks than we figured. But first, I'd like to prove my theory about these footprints. Let's follow the marks."

The group had no difficulty doing this. The prints were visible as far as Eddy Run. Here they vanished and there were no imprints of any kind, bird or human, along the shoreline.

"Maybe the spook can fly," George quipped.

As the group turned back toward Ivy Hall, Nancy's eyes swept the entire area. Suddenly she dashed off a short distance and picked up an object embedded in the mud. "I've found the answer!" she exclaimed exultantly.

Coming back to the others, Nancy showed them a bronze cast of a peacock's foot with straps attached.

"It must have dropped off the man's shoe," she said. "I presume this birdman came and went in a boat, so there's no chance of following him."

As the group walked back to the house everyone discussed this new angle of the mystery. But when they reached Ivy Hall, Sheila insisted that all sleuthing cease for the day. "This is the strangest Sunday I have ever spent in my life," she said. "I think we all should have a little spiritual uplift!"

"But I don't feel," said Annette, "that we should leave the house for long."

Sheila nodded. With dramatic steps she marched to an old-time organ in the parlor, opened it, and began to play hymns. Though it wheezed a bit and some notes did not sound, the girls managed to keep in tune and joined her in singing for over an hour. The serene atmosphere was relaxing and the mood remained until bedtime. Then Sheila began to worry again.

"I won't sleep a wink," she said, "unless everything in Ivy Hall is nailed tight shut. There seem to be all kinds of entrances to this old house that we can't find but others can use. The ghost must have come through that basement window, and we didn't even know it was there."

Nancy agreed that this was true. She suggested that the regular cellar doors be securely bolted, the secret entrance to the tunnel nailed shut, and the trap door in the attic covered with a heavy trunk.

"And I'll disconnect the mechanism in the wall," she said. Taking a flashlight and a screw driver she went to the third floor and deftly removed the spring and lever.

Returning to the others, she remarked, "If we hear footsteps in this house tonight, Sheila, I'll almost agree with you that our visitor is supernatural."

Everyone went to bed early and soon fell asleep. Nancy, with the various mysteries on her mind, woke up at about midnight. Wondering why, she listened intently. There was not a sound in the old house. Smiling to herself, the girl detective turned over and fell asleep once more.

Some time later she woke again. There was no mistaking the reason this time. Outside her window she heard screeching sounds. They were the same as those she had heard coming from inside the walls of Cumberland Manor! Jumping from her cot, Nancy looked out the window. She could see nothing on the lawn below.

By now the screeching had awakened Bess and George. "How horrible!" Bess cried out. "Where is it?"

She and her cousin hopped out of bed and hurried to Nancy's side. Still nothing could be seen outside.

"I'm going down to find out what's going on!" Nancy said.

As she pulled on bathrobe and slippers, George said she and Bess would go along. Nancy grabbed her flashlight and hurried to the first floor. She swung open the front door and rushed down the steps, beaming her light ahead of her.

In its glare stood a magnificent peacock, its fan fully spread!

"Oh!" Bess exclaimed. "The story's true!"

At that moment Sheila and Annette appeared on the porch. When the actress saw the bird, she cried out in terror, then fainted. As Sheila slumped to the floor, Bess and Annette caught her and carried the unconscious woman indoors.

"Don't worry, girls," said Annette. "Mother often does this." George remained with Nancy.

The girl detective, meanwhile, had swung her flashlight in a wide arc over the area beyond the peacock. For a fraction of a second Nancy thought she glimpsed the figure of a crouching man, but when she turned the light back, he was gone.

By this time the peacock had recovered from the hypnotism caused by the light shining directly in his eyes. Folding his tail, he began to run across the lawn.

"Let's follow him, George!" Nancy whispered, keeping her flashlight trained on him.

The bird ran faster than the girls had any idea he could. They had a hard time keeping up with the peacock as they followed him across a field.

"He's going into the woods!" George said suddenly. "We may lose track of him!"

The girls ran even faster, their robes flapping in the slight breeze that had sprung up. The peacock followed a path among the trees, which ended at Eddy Run. Now the bird turned left along the shore. Sloshing through the mud, Nancy and George kept pace with him.

"I wonder how far he's going?" George asked. She chuckled and added, "I've been on some crazy chases with you, Nancy Drew, but this one's the prize!"

Nancy agreed that it did seem absurd to be chasing a peacock at this hour. "If my hunch that he's going to Cumberland Manor is wrong," she said, laughing, "I'll carry you back home. But we're not far from Mr. Honsho's estate now and maybe——"

As she spoke, the peacock disappeared. Apparently he had run behind a high mass of bushes. Nancy started around the corner of the tangled shrubbery, with George close behind. Holding the flashlight directly in front of her, Nancy hoped to catch sight of the big bird again.

Instead, the light picked up a white-sheeted figure!

"The ghost!" George exclaimed.

If the masquerader had hoped to frighten the two girls into fleeing, he failed. Instead, they ran directly toward the figure, which took to its heels around the shrubbery and vanished.

Nancy and George continued the search, but their advance was suddenly halted a few minutes later. A stream of water hit both girls in the face full force. It knocked them to the ground and Nancy's flashlight went out!

CHAPTER XV

A Worrisome Gift

THE stream of water that had knocked Nancy and George to the ground suddenly stopped. Thoroughly drenched, the two girls got to their feet. Nancy located her flashlight and turned it on. Both the bird and the white-sheeted figure were gone. Nancy shined her light around the area. Suddenly it illuminated a brick wall.

"Cumberland Manor's just ahead," she remarked. "There must be a gate in this side of the wall. By now the ghost and the peacock are inside."

"Where did that water come from?" George asked.

"Since the force was so strong, I imagine someone inside the grounds used a fire hose," replied Nancy.

The girls followed the trail of water, which led directly to a gate.

"I think Luke's trying to get even with Annette because she won't date him," George remarked. "He let the peacock loose in Ivy Hall to scare her and the rest of us."

George went on to say she thought Luke had not expected anyone to follow him and the peacock. When the two girls ran after them, Luke had taken another means of trying to frighten them. When even the ghost disguise did not work, he turned the hose on them in desperation.

"Luke Seeny also might be the one who strapped the peacock's feet onto his shoes and who played ghost in the house," Nancy added.

"Exactly," George agreed.

Nancy still was convinced the masquerader was after a valuable object in Ivy Hall. "Let's find out more about Luke tomorrow," she suggested.

Since the gate to Cumberland Manor was locked, the girls decided to return to Ivy Hall. The brilliance of the moonlight made traveling so easy that Nancy turned off her flashlight. They walked along the bank of Eddy Run. Suddenly Nancy grabbed George and pulled her behind a clump of bushes.

The young sleuth pointed to a lone figure in a canoe. "If we're wrong about Luke Seeny, that man may be the ghost," she said.

"It's Alonzo Rugby!" George whispered.

Nancy was perplexed. If Rugby had been playing ghost, he had certainly made excellent time, getting from the gate of Cumberland Manor into a canoe on Eddy Run. She mentioned this to George and added, "Maybe Alonzo and Luke are in cahoots!"

"Where do you figure Rugby's going?" George asked. "And where did he come from?"

"He may be coming from Bradshaw's studio," Nancy guessed. "Maybe it's a coincidence that we've seen him tonight. He might not have anything to do with Cumberland Manor or Luke Seeny."

The two girls started off again and twenty minutes later reached Ivy Hall. Sheila was nearly beside herself with worry about them.

"Thank goodness you're here," the actress said. "What happened to you?" she asked, noticing their wet clothes. She insisted that they change into dry pajamas before explaining.

Ten minutes later the group gathered in Sheila's bedroom, where Bess and the Pattersons listened to the story of the girls' adventure. When they finished, Annette said she would phone the hotel in the morning to find out more about Luke.

At nine o'clock the following day, she called and learned that Luke did have a room there. He had left right after breakfast.

"Would you mind telling me," Annette said in an exaggerated coaxing drawl, "whether Mr. Seeny was in the hotel last night?"

"I'm sorry, but we don't keep track of our guests' comings and goings."

After Annette had hung up, she reported to the others, adding, "I guess I'm not much good as a detective."

Nancy smiled. "I'd say you did a grand job. Our next project is to find out something about our other suspect, Alonzo Rugby. Let's drive to the farmhouse where he lives."

"Please don't be gone long," Sheila requested.

"We'll be back by lunchtime," Nancy promised.

She drove off with Bess and George, and headed for Uplands Road. Reaching it, she slowed down to look at the name on each mailbox. Coming to one marked Paget, she turned into the lane leading to the rambling farmhouse.

When the car stopped near the kitchen door, a slender, gray-haired woman came outside. Nancy asked her if Mr. Rugby was at home.

"No, he's not here and he hasn't been here for a week. He stops in once in a while for mail, but he never eats or sleeps here any more," Mrs. Paget answered.

"Have you any idea where he's staying?" Nancy prodded.

"Well, I suppose he's staying with that Mr. Bradshaw he works for—or isn't he?"

"I don't know," Nancy replied. "I'm from River Heights, where his sister lives. In fact, she's a neighbor of mine."

"How do you like her?" the woman asked.

"Well," Nancy answered, "Mrs. Dondo hasn't been very friendly toward me and my family. I heard she had a brother living in Charlottesville and I'm curious to meet him."

"She lived here in Charlottesville, you know," Mrs. Paget continued, "and my, what a busy-body she was! Things got so bad she came near being sued."

"Oh, really?" Bess asked. "What did she do?"

"She accused people of things they never did."

"Like what?" George asked.

"Well," Mrs. Paget replied, "It seems that Mrs. Dondo was expecting a letter with some money in it. When it didn't arrive, she spoke to the postman. He said it might have got mixed in with other people's mail. So Mrs. Dondo up and goes around asking everybody. Then she accused a woman she didn't like of keeping the money."

Nancy and her friends were amazed. It was the same trick Mrs. Dondo tried in River Heights.

"I understand," said Nancy nonchalantly, "that Mr. Rugby has a lot of money and is very generous in helping his sister."

Mrs. Paget began to laugh. "Money! Neither one of them has got any money to speak of, but they both go around putting on airs."

The girls smiled. They were getting more information than they had hoped for!

"Alonzo's not so bad," Mrs. Paget added. "The only thing I got against him is his bragging. He thinks he's a great artist."

Mrs. Paget stopped to take a breath, and then went on, "What makes you think Alonzo sends his sister any money? If you ask me, he never gave her a nickel in his life!" Suddenly Mrs. Paget sniffed. "Oh, my goodness!" she cried. "My dinner must be burned to a crisp!"

With that, she dashed toward the house. Nancy called after her, "I'm afraid we must leave now, Mrs. Paget, but we enjoyed meeting you."

"Thank you—call again!" the woman yelled back from inside the kitchen.

Nancy remarked that she could hardly wait to get to a telephone and relay the recent conversation to her father. She suggested that they stop at Susan's home, which they would pass. "I'd like to say hello, anyway."

The girls were disappointed not to find either Susan or Cliff at home. But Anna warmly welcomed them back. Hearing that they were not staying, she threw up her hands and exclaimed, "Why don't you all remain here now that you're back safe?"

Nancy smiled. "Don't worry, we'll be home again in no time."

Anna sighed and shook her head in disappointment. Nancy phoned Mr. Drew, and Bess followed the housekeeper to the kitchen. "Anna," she said as she took a seat, "the worst thing about our mystery solving at Ivy Hall is not being able to enjoy your delicious cooking. No one can match *your* recipes!"

Anna burst into laughter. "I can spot a hint from a hungry girl a mile away," she said. She cut Bess a large slice of coconut cake.

"Thank you," Bess exclaimed happily and started eating with gusto.

As she finished the last bite, a car stopped in the driveway. Susan stepped from it, waved good-by, and came into the kitchen.

"Bess!" she cried in delight. "I'm so glad to see you! But where are George and Nancy?"

Bess told her, then Susan said, "I was just thinking of you girls and the Pattersons." She turned to Anna. "I'd like to have the girls take a basket of food with them. With all the excitement at Ivy Hall, it would help if Sheila didn't have to cook dinners for a couple of days."

"A good idea, Miss Susan," Anna said and went to pack a picnic hamper.

"And now, tell me what has happened since you left there," Susan said to Bess, linking arms and leading her into the living room.

Nancy and George joined them and the four sat down. Susan listened intently as the others related their story. At the end Susan remarked, "It all seems unbelievable. I think the mystery is becoming more dangerous each day."

"And nearer a solution," Nancy declared. She rose. "We must get back to our sleuthing."

As the girls drove off, Susan said, "Don't forget we're going on a tour of the gardens tomorrow. Pick me up early."

Nancy said she would and waved good-by. At Ivy Hall the girls found Sheila and Annette in a flutter of excitement. A messenger boy had just been there to deliver a long, narrow box, attractively wrapped, with Annette's name on it.

Excited, the girl raised the lid. Directly underneath lay a note, which she instantly read. Her face clouded. "It's from Luke. He's pleading that I make a date with him."

"Let's see what he sent," George said.

Annette finished unwrapping the gift.

Sheila shrieked. "A peacock fan! Oh, no, more bad luck!"

Though Bess looked worried, Nancy and George did not take Sheila's outburst seriously, and they asked Annette to spread open the fan.

"This is exquisite," Nancy remarked.

Annette was impressed with the gift, yet she could not bring herself to make a date with the sender of the fan.

"He's still a 'ghost' prospect," George observed.

Nancy suddenly exclaimed, "Annette, I want you to make a date with Luke Seeny!"

"Why?"

"I think if you invite Luke here, we may solve the mystery," Nancy replied.

Sheila said disapprovingly, "I don't want my daughter associating with such a person. What's more, I insist that Annette return this fan."

"Just a moment, Mother," Annette said. "First let's hear what Nancy's plan is."

"All right," Sheila conceded. "What is it you want Annette to do, Nancy?"

"Invite Luke here to dinner tomorrow evening," the young sleuth replied. "I think we can trap him into telling the truth!"

CHAPTER XVI

A Wonderful Discovery

AFTER some deliberation Sheila Patterson finally consented to Nancy's plan. She was still worried and reluctant to have Luke around.

"Don't be concerned," said George. "If anyone can set a trap for that cowboy, Nancy can!"

"That's right," Bess agreed. "And we have another surprise for you!" She went out to the car and brought in the hamper of food.

On seeing what it contained, Sheila cried. "The people around here have been so kind," she said. "It makes me feel bad that I'm not in a position to return their favors."

"I'm sure you can," said Bess. "Everyone would certainly love to see you act. Perhaps you could put on a performance for them."

Sheila admitted she had already been asked by Susan Carr to put on a skit for a charity performance in a few weeks. "I really haven't felt up to it," the actress said. "But now you give me a new incentive, Bess. I'll do it!"

"And I'd like to entertain here," said Annette wistfully, "if the grounds were only fixed up."

After lunch George proposed that the group tidy up the grounds. The Pattersons were delighted and the rest of the day was spent working with lawn mowers, rakes, spades, and shovels. By suppertime the grass, flower beds, and shrubbery looked trim and well-kept.

Sheila smiled in delight. "Isn't it beautiful?" she said. "I love this place, really. If only the mystery of Ivy Hall could be cleared up!"

"I have a hunch," said Nancy, "that it won't be long before the ghost is caught. Annette, will you call Luke now?"

Annette went inside to phone. She returned a few minutes later, saying that Luke would be there the following evening.

The night passed without incident. Sheila was in good spirits the next morning and did not object when Nancy set off early with Bess and George to pick up Susan for the Garden Tour. "I know you'll love it," she said.

The weather was perfect. The visitors gasped in admiration at the show gardens with their magnificent flowering shrubs and beautiful flowers.

Toward the end of the afternoon Susan directed her friends to one of the oldest estates in the vicinity. She told them that the present owner, Mr. Van Buskirk, had bought the place intact, and all the servants had remained.

"There's one old woman here you'll love," Susan said. "She's quite infirm and spends most of her time in a rocking chair. But she has a fabulous memory and loves to tell stories of the old South. She may be able to give you some helpful information, Nancy."

The young detective was thrilled. After she and her friends had admired the creamy-pink flowering magnolias, the lavender-tinted plum blossoms, and the extensive boxwood-enclosed beds of azaleas and tulips, they went to the old slave quarters. The Van Buskirks had modernized them as accommodations for their servants.

Susan knocked on one of the doors. It was opened by a slight, stooped, white-haired woman.

"Howdy, Mrs. Carr," she said in a low, soft voice.

"Hello, Mrs. Johnson. I've brought some friends of mine from the North," Susan said. "They'd like to ask you a few questions."

"Please come in, young ladies," the elderly woman invited.

Susan introduced the girls and everyone sat down. "Miss Drew is a detective," Susan explained. "She's trying to find some trace of a family who may have lived around here. Their name was Greystone."

Mrs. Johnson put one hand to her forehead as if thinking hard. Finally she said, "I never heard of a family named Greystone, but I did know about one called Grayce. Do you suppose, Miss Drew, that they might have changed their name when they came to America?"

Nancy was excited to hear this. "You say when they came to America? Where did the Grayce family come from?"

"It was England," Mrs. Johnson replied. "I say maybe they changed their name, 'cause my folks told me that when Mrs. Grayce was dying, she cried out, 'Please forgive us, Lord Greystone. We were wrong to come here!' "

Startled, the callers stared at one another. Nancy quickly calculated that Mrs. Johnson's great-grandmother might well have lived around 1850!

"Where is the Grayce family now?" Nancy asked.

"Oh, they all died off long ago," Mrs. Johnson said sadly.

There was a moment of sympathetic silence. Then Nancy asked, "Mrs. Johnson, did your mother ever tell you that the Grayce family had a stained-glass window in their home?"

The old woman shook her head. "But if there was one, maybe it's still there. Why don't you go look for it?"

"Where is the house?" Nancy asked, her heart

thumping wildly as she waited for the answer.

Mrs. Johnson said the place was only a few miles away. "It's called—let me think—oh yes, I remember now. It's Ivy Hall."

"Hypers!" George cried out.

The old woman looked at the girl in surprise. George quickly explained that the visitors were staying at Ivy Hall.

"We hunted for a window there," Nancy said, "but we'll search again. Thank you for telling us about the Grayce family."

As the group headed for Susan's home, the conversation was full of speculation. Were the Grayce and Greystone families one and the same?

If so, was Ivy Hall, the former Grayce home, the original property of the Greystones from England? Had the stained-glass window once been there? And was it hidden there now?

Finally George chuckled. "I suppose, Nancy, that now you'll want to tear the place down brick by brick to find out."

Her friend smiled. "I'm hoping Luke Seeny will spare us the trouble."

After they had dropped Susan at Seven Oaks, the girls reviewed their campaign for the evening. Each one was to play a part in trying to trick Luke into revealing whether or not he had been the ghost.

Annette's guest, immaculately dressed, arrived

at seven o'clock. He was poised and polite. Luke was greeted in a very friendly fashion and seemed pleased to meet the girls from River Heights.

"I'm sure that he's not suspicious of us," Nancy thought.

Conversation remained light until dessert was served. Then Bess asked the visitor if he knew Alonzo Rugby.

"No, I never heard of him," Luke replied.

Nancy, watching the cowboy closely, was convinced he was telling the truth. Presently George brought up the subject of Garden Week and remarked that everyone in the area was disappointed that Mr. Honsho would not open his estate to the public. "Why won't he?" she asked.

Luke frowned. "I don't know. He's kind of a recluse—doesn't have much to do with people who live around these parts. When he heard I was visiting here from Oklahoma, he sent for me. Said he wanted to find out all about my home state."

"Oh, you don't work for him?" Nancy asked. "We noticed that you had a key to the estate."

The young man reddened. "Mr. Honsho never leaves the grounds," he replied. "He gave me a key."

Bess sighed. "It must be beautiful behind those brick walls," she said. "Tell me about it, Luke."

"Not much to tell," he replied. "There are nice flowers, trees, and bushes. That's all."

Nancy mentioned the strange sounds the girls had heard coming from Cumberland Manor. Looking straight at Luke, she asked, "Does Mr. Honsho keep peacocks?"

For the first time, Luke appeared nervous. He did not reply at once. When he did, he merely said, "I'm not privileged to discuss Mr. Honsho's private business."

But Nancy was inwardly exulting. Luke's reaction to the mention of peacocks must have some bearing on the mystery!

When the meal was over, Annette asked Luke if he would like to see the house and some of its secrets. The young man's eyes popped wide open as he answered, "Indeed I would!"

Annette grinned impishly. Turning to the three girls, she said, "You and Mother must come too. I think you'd enjoy seeing some of the things."

This was all part of the prearranged plan to trap Luke, but Nancy, Bess, and George were thunderstruck when Annette led them to the old library and removed a section of the built-in bookcase. Behind it was a wall safe, its combination lock gone. There was nothing in the safe.

"I guess the former owners took everything out of here," Annette remarked.

Luke showed great surprise and interest in the hiding place. Was he faking?

Annette now led the group into the kitchen, where she tugged at one of the hearthstones and lifted it. To the amazement of the visiting girls, and apparently Luke, a very narrow stairway was revealed.

"I think it was a storage room," said Sheila. "There's nothing down there now but a lot of empty bottles."

Annette said that during the day, when the three girls had been away, she and her mother had instituted a search of Ivy Hall.

"The next place I want to show you, Luke," said Annette, "is our attic."

All eyes watched the guest closely. They were sure that this time he gave an involuntary start.

When the group reached the third floor, George adroitly steered Luke toward the trunk from which the girls were sure the ghost had removed a sheet.

"Luke Seeny, this is the hide-out of Ivy Hall's ghost," George intoned in a sepulchral voice.

The girls laughed and Annette said, "Our tour is almost over, Luke, so don't worry."

She locked an arm into his and guided him toward the trap door, from which the trunk had been removed. Pausing directly on top of the door, she pointed out an antique water jug.

"Isn't it quaint?" she asked.

In the meantime, Nancy had moved to the side wall and was now pushing back the secret panel. "Luke," she said, "there's a lever back here that——"

A look of terror came over the young man's face. "Don't touch it!" he yelled. "Don't you dare touch it!"

Luke jumped off the trap door, dragging Annette with him!

CHAPTER XVII

A Ghost Confesses

"So you're the ghost of Ivy Hall!" Nancy cried triumphantly.

Luke kept silent.

"You work for Mr. Honsho and brought a peacock from his place over here the other night, didn't you?" George accused him.

"I told you before I wouldn't discuss Mr. Honsho," Luke said defiantly. "What is this? The third degree?"

Nancy smiled and said in a coaxing manner, "It's no use, Luke. There's too much evidence against you—your knowledge of the mechanism that opens the trap door, your leaving the trunk open after you took the sheet out of it, the bronze peacock's foot strapped to your own shoes—and lost in the mud——"

"Don't say any more!" Luke begged. "I don't know how you found out all those things. You're a pretty smart girl, but I haven't done anything wrong—really I haven't."

"Suppose you tell us the whole story," Nancy suggested. "We'll go downstairs and sit in some comfortable chairs."

"And you won't call the police?" the young man asked fearfully.

Sheila Patterson spoke up. "We'll answer that question when we've heard your story."

By the time they were seated in the old parlor of Ivy Hall, Luke seemed completely crestfallen. He was very pale, and as he began to speak, his voice shook.

"I worked as a cowboy in Oklahoma. My parents had no money and the only cash I ever had was what I earned. I saved a little and decided to try my luck here.

"What I told you about Mr. Honsho getting in touch with me," Luke continued, "was pretty near the truth. Right after I got here, the hotel manager asked me if I'd like a job. When I said yes, he told me that Mr. Honsho was looking for somebody to help around his place. I rented a bicycle and rode out there."

The Oklahoman went on to say that while working at Cumberland Manor he had found an old diary that belonged to a former owner of the estate. In it he had found a notation that mentioned that there was a very unusual stained-glass window on the neighboring property.

"That same day I happened to see an article in a copy of *Continental* magazine, which contained Sir Richard Greystone's offer to the finder of a certain stained-glass window. I thought the window might be hidden at Ivy Hall, and I decided to find out."

Luke hung his head. "First I tried to date Annette so that I could get a good look at the inside of the house. When she refused, I figured the only way to find out about the window was to get inside the place somehow. I decided to try scaring the Pattersons away by bringing over one of Mr. Honsho's peacocks—he has a flock of them."

Annette looked at the young man in disgust. "You nearly succeeded in driving us out," she said. "If it hadn't been for Nancy Drew, we probably wouldn't be here tonight."

"Please go on with your story, Luke," Nancy urged.

The cowboy said that after he had failed to scare the Pattersons away, he had risked entering the old house at night. He had become pretty well acquainted with it, even to finding the mechanism that worked the trap door.

"So they were your footsteps we heard!" Annette remarked.

Luke nodded. When the girls had nearly discovered him in the attic, he had hidden behind the secret panel. He had seized the opportunity to open the trap door and send Nancy and George down the slide, convinced that this would frighten the group away from Ivy Hall.

Luke said he had used the slide himself previously and had found the secret opening into the kitchen. He had figured that the two girls would also locate it and escape.

Bess interrupted Luke to ask, "Why did you nearly scare me out of my wits, playing ghost in the attic? You could have stayed behind the panel until I left."

"I suppose I could have," Luke replied. "But you just seemed like the scary type and I thought my trick would drive you all away."

"And you played the same trick," George said, "when Nancy and I chased you and the peacock over to Cumberland Manor."

Luke admitted that he had taken the sheet along and hidden it in some bushes. When his attempt to scare Nancy and George had failed, he had turned Mr. Honsho's fire hose on them.

"I guess I'm just a good-for-nothing," the cowboy said. "But I don't want to go to jail. Please don't call the police," he begged again.

Nancy said this decision lay with the Pattersons. "What I'd like to know is, Did you find any clue to the missing peacock window?"

"No, I didn't," Luke said. "You've got to believe me."

He looked pleadingly at Sheila Patterson. She

was silent for a minute then said, "I suppose we all make mistakes, especially if we're trying too hard to make quick money."

Luke looked relieved. "I'll tell you what," he burst out. "To show you I'm on the level, I'll take you all over to Cumberland Manor and introduce you to Mr. Honsho. Then you can ask him to open his place for Garden Week."

The unexpected offer surprised the group so much that for a moment no one answered Luke.

Then Nancy spoke. "When do you want us to go?" she asked.

"Why, right away," he answered. "Mr. Honsho doesn't go to bed until very late."

Nancy relaxed. It began to look as if Luke Seeny were not a malicious character—but a weak person who could not resist temptation.

"We'll go," Nancy said. She led the way out to the car and the whole group piled in.

When they reached Cumberland Manor, Nancy parked, and the party walked down the path lighted by the beam of Nancy's flashlight. After Luke had unlocked the gate, the visitors stepped inside and the young man carefully locked it again.

"Follow me," he said, and led the way among towering trees and lovely gardens to the old stone mansion. It was English Tudor in style, and the lights within seemed to beckon the visitors hospitably.

Luke gave a peculiar whistle to announce their approach. After he had repeated it a second time, the front door of the mansion opened. A slender man of medium build, with dark skin and hair, came outside.

"Mr. Honsho," Luke called out, "I've brought you some visitors."

Although the callers realized that the Indian gentleman must be very much surprised and perhaps annoyed, he gave no evidence of it. Cordially he invited them into the house, which was furnished exquisitely. Luke introduced the visitors one by one and told Mr. Honsho where they were from, adding that the Pattersons had recently bought Ivy Hall.

"I am pleased to meet you all," said their host. He spoke flawless English with a British accent. Then he turned to Luke and with a smile said, "I presume the visitors have learned our little secret?"

"Yes, they have, sir," Luke replied. "Miss Drew is an amateur detective. She recognized the screeching of the peacocks."

Mr. Honsho looked at the girl in combined perplexity and admiration. He made no comment on the subject, however. Instead, he said, "Is it because of my peacocks that I have the honor of your visit this evening?"

"Not entirely," said Nancy. "I'm a cousin of Mrs. Clifford Carr's, one of your neighbors.

She's on the Garden Week committee. Because I love to solve mysteries, she asked me if I would try to find out why you refused to open your gardens to the public."

Mr. Honsho chuckled. "And you know the answer? That I would not do it because I heard some people in this area are superstitious about peacocks?"

Nancy smiled. "Whatever I thought, I did not mention it to anyone. But I assure you, Mr. Honsho, you have perhaps been misinformed about Americans believing that peacocks bring bad luck. Most of us, like people in your country, think the birds are very beautiful and we admire them."

The Indian's face broke into a broad smile. "I am relieved to hear that," he said, "because I am very proud of my beautiful birds. Come, I will show them to you."

After turning on several switches, which lighted the grounds, he led the way back of the house to an extensive wire enclosure. In it, roosting among the trees, were a large number of birds. Mr. Honsho made a low cooing sound and instantly one of them left its roost and flew down to him. It was pure white and very stately.

"This bird is sacred to us Indians," Mr. Honsho said, gazing affectionately at the beautiful feathered creature. "If you can assure me, Miss Drew, that visitors to my place will not injure my peacocks, I will be happy to open my gates."

The girls expressed their thanks and voiced their admiration of his proud-looking birds. "I hope every one of them will spread its fan when the sightseers come," said Bess.

Mr. Honsho bade his callers good night, adding that he would leave the lights on until Luke had escorted the group outside the gate.

"Isn't Mr. Honsho charming?" Bess burst out as they drove off. "And so different from what I expected."

"He's been very good to me," said Luke. On the way back to Ivy Hall, the cowboy was silent until they reached the house. Then he asked apprehensively, "Have I cleared myself?"

Sheila looked at him steadily. Then she said, "Luke, I think maybe you've learned your lesson. I won't prosecute you."

Meanwhile, Annette had gone into the house and now came out with the feather fan. "I want you to take this with you," she said, handing it to Luke.

A look of pain crossed his face. "I made it for you myself," he said. "Please keep the fan. It'll help to make up for all the trouble I've caused."

"Well, if you insist. And thank you," the girl answered.

Luke expressed his gratitude to the group for their leniency toward him, hopped on his bicycle, and pedaled off into the darkness.

As the girls from River Heights were preparing for bed, George patted Nancy on the shoulder. "Congratulations, old pal. You've solved one of the mysteries of Charlottesville!"

Nancy grinned. Now she could concentrate on the others. She was the first one up the following morning and at once telephoned Susan Carr.

"Hi, Sue!" she said. "Good news! Mr. Honsho is going to open his gardens to visitors this morning and for the rest of Garden Week!"

Susan exclaimed, "I don't know how you did it!" Nancy briefly told her what had happened.

Susan said she would notify the rest of the committee at once and each of them would make phone calls to spread the word that Cumberland Manor would be open to the public.

The group at Ivy Hall had a quick breakfast and set off immediately for Mr. Honsho's estate. He greeted them cordially and said that Luke had come directly back to Cumberland Manor after leaving the girls. He had worked all night to get the place ready for display.

The Indian told them that Luke had confessed everything, including taking the peacock. He felt the young man sincerely regretted his actions. Nancy and her friends were glad to hear this.

They spent the whole day welcoming the many visitors to the Cumberland Manor gardens. Men and women especially admired the exquisite peacocks. To the delight of the crowd, many of the birds strutted around with their fans spread.

It was late in the afternoon when Nancy and her friends returned to Ivy Hall. All were weary and declared that as soon as supper was over, they were going to bed.

"I'm warning everybody now," said Nancy, "that I'm getting up at the crack of dawn to hunt for the stained-glass window."

"I'll be with you," said George, and Bess nodded her agreement.

By this time Sheila had unlocked the great front door and the group walked in.

Suddenly the actress shrieked. "Oh, my home! My home!" she cried out.

Everyone stared in stupefied amazement at what they saw. Walls, floors, and ceilings had been hacked. The place was a shambles!

CHAPTER XVIII

Rifled Luggage

SHEILA Patterson became so hysterical that the girls forgot everything else. The actress alternately laughed and cried, and continuously pointed to the hacked walls, floor, and ceilings.

"We must call a doctor," said Annette. She was on the verge of hysterics herself.

George hurried to the phone while the others endeavored to calm Sheila, but this was impossible. There was nothing to do except wait for Dr. Tillett to come.

"We must notify the police also," Nancy said, and phoned headquarters immediately.

Two officers arrived at the same time Dr. Tillett did. Sheila was put to bed and a short while later the physician announced that she was asleep. By morning, he said, the actress would have recovered from her shock.

In the meantime, Nancy had answered all the

questions the police had asked, then had shown them through the house. They found that entry had been made by smashing a dining-room window. The various secret places of the mansion were revealed and investigated. There was no clue to the intruder.

One of the officers, named Hanley, said, "The fellow must have worn gloves and there are no distinct footprints."

The two policemen had about concluded their work when Bess cried out from the girls' bedroom. Nancy and the officers rushed to see what the trouble was.

"That horrible burglar," Bess exclaimed, "mussed up all our clothes!" She explained that upon opening her suitcase she had found everything in it in disorder. "And my beautiful new slip is gone!" Bess added woefully.

Quickly Nancy's and George's baggage was examined. Their suitcases, too, were in disarray, and several new articles of lingerie were missing.

Officer Hanley frowned. "That's strange burglarizing," he remarked. "Why anyone would hack up a house and then steal women's clothes doesn't make sense. But there's one answer. Two intruders—a man and a woman—may have been here."

The policemen examined the room for clues to establish this. Finally Officer Hanley admitted that there were none.

"We'll report our findings to the chief," he told the girls.

After the men left, Nancy and George boarded up the window the intruder had smashed. Then they made sure everything was locked tightly before going to their room. Bess, already in bed, asked if Nancy had any theories as to the person who had been in the house.

"Well, Luke Seeny is exonerated," Nancy replied, "which pinpoints the suspect as Alonzo Rugby."

"Do you think there was any reason for rifling our suitcases, except to steal the lingerie?"

"Yes, I do, Bess. I believe Rugby was looking for letters I might have had from Lord Greystone regarding the peacock window."

"Then you don't think a woman was here too?" George inquired.

Nancy shrugged. Suddenly she smiled. "Maybe one of these days Alonzo Rugby's loving sister will be wearing our brand-new lingerie!"

"Ugh!" Bess said.

George turned out the light and soon the girls were asleep. The next morning they found Sheila feeling well and in complete control of her emotions. She said that damage to the house was covered by insurance, and she would attend to having repairs made as soon as possible.

After breakfast Nancy announced that she was going to make an even more exhaustive search of the house. "First I'm going to look for clues to the hidden window. Then I hope to learn, if possible, whether or not the burglar discovered the window and took it away."

All four girls joined in the search, but two hours later they admitted defeat. They sat down in the living room with Sheila to discuss what to do next.

"Well, I know what I'm going to do," said George, rising. "Go upstairs and wash my hair. It's so full of dust, I can't stand it."

She left the others and climbed the steps. Halfway up she stopped short, leaned down, and picked up a small piece of oblong-shaped dark-red glass. Excited, George hurried down the stairs and showed it to the others.

"Do you suppose the burglar dropped this?" she asked.

Nancy took the piece of glass and held it up to the light. The glass was wavy and looked very old. "Probably someone familiar with leaded windows dropped this," she said.

Sheila burst into tears. "Oh, that dreadful man did find our stained-glass window! Now there won't be a reward for any of us or a chance to sell the window!"

Nancy had to admit it would be pretty difficult to prove that the old window had been stolen from Ivy Hall. The finder could easily say it had been found someplace else. Then, suddenly, a

"Do you suppose the burglar dropped this?"
George asked.

new thought came to her. Maybe the red glass was not part of the window they were searching for!

"There's still hope, Sheila," she said kindly, and told then what she suspected.

"You think this man Rugby dropped the piece of glass?" Annette asked.

Nancy nodded. "I'm going to find out, if I possibly can, where Rugby is staying and where he was yesterday."

"How are you going to do that?" Sheila questioned.

"I'll enlist my cousin Susan's aid," Nancy replied. "I'll ask Sue to call Mrs. Bradshaw and casually ask if Rugby is their house guest."

Going to the phone, she called the Carr home. When Susan answered, she told her what had happened at Ivy Hall.

"How dreadful!" Susan said. "That lovely old house! I'll find out right away what you want to know and call you, Nancy."

The return call came ten minutes later. Alonzo Rugby had not been staying with the Bradshaws and had not slept in the studio, either. Mrs. Bradshaw did not know where the man had been the day before, because she and her husband had gone on a tour of gardens, and assumed that Rugby had worked in the studio all day as usual.

"Thanks, Sue," Nancy said.

"Glad to help, Nancy. And let me know if I can do anything else."

Nancy returned to the living room and said, "Rugby had a marvelous opportunity to spend hours here yesterday. I think we should do some sleuthing and see if we can find out where he's staying."

She outlined her plan. The girls would get a canoe and hide it on Eddy Run near Bradshaw's studio.

"If Alonzo leaves in a car, we'll follow him with ours. But if he goes off in a canoe, we'll trail him on the water."

Once more Susan Carr's aid was enlisted. She borrowed a canoe for Nancy, and Cliff brought it over in the station wagon. The girls carried it Indian-style down to the stream and paddled it up near Waverly. They hid the canoe among some bushes, then walked back to Ivy Hall.

"What time do you think we should start our spying?" George asked Nancy.

The young sleuth felt that there was no necessity to do anything before five o'clock, the time that Rugby normally left the studio. Sheila prepared an early supper for the girls; then they set off in the car.

After parking near the driveway into Waverly, they walked through the woods bordering the road, down to the studio. From among the trees they could easily look into the building. Rugby was moving about but showed no signs of leaving.

"We may have a long wait," said Nancy. "I really hope he doesn't leave until after dark."

As if acceding to her wish, Rugby stayed inside the studio. As hour after hour went by, Bess became tired of the vigil and suggested that they leave.

"I wouldn't think of it," said George firmly, and Nancy agreed.

As darkness came, the girls moved closer to the studio. The windows were open and they could hear Rugby mumbling to himself. There was only one small light in the studio. This was near the telephone.

Presently Rugby consulted his watch. Then he picked up the telephone and gave a number in New York City.

"Whom do you suppose he's calling?" Bess whispered.

The other two girls did not reply, for just then the operator made the connection and Alonzo Rugby began to speak. "Is this Sir Richard Greystone?"

The three girls gripped one another's arms as the suspect went on, "You will? That's great. I'm certainly glad you're going to fly down. The old peacock window is in perfect condition, Sir Richard. Wait until you see it!"

The listeners were stunned. Apparently Alonzo

Rugby had found the missing window. Had he stolen it from Ivy Hall? Would he get the reward for locating it, and perhaps even sell the window to Sir Richard Greystone?

"Isn't this awful!" Bess exclaimed in a whisper.

As soon as Rugby had completed his phone call, he flicked off the light, came to the door, and walked outside. He locked the studio, lighted a cigarette, and set off for Eddy Run.

"Come on!" said Nancy.

Quiet as mice, the girls trailed him. Reaching the water, the man stepped into a canoe and paddled off. His pursuers broke into a run, launched their own craft, and climbed in. With Nancy in the prow and George in the stern they paddled after the suspect.

Rugby, familiar with the stream, zigzagged among the rocks. Nancy and George tried to follow his course but found this impossible.

Suddenly the girls' canoe rammed a stone. There was a splintering sound and within moments water gushed into the craft!

CHAPTER XIX

Captured!

"WHAT LUCK!" George exclaimed in disgust.

Further pursuit of Alonzo was impossible. He was already out of sight. The girls paddled their rapidly filling canoe as close to land as they could, then waded ashore, pulling the craft after them.

"This thing is a wreck," said Bess. "We'd better win that reward so we can pay for it."

Wet and discouraged, the girls plodded back to their car and returned to Ivy Hall. The Pattersons were overwhelmed by the news regarding the stained-glass window.

"I told you peacocks bring bad luck!" Sheila said. "No one ever had any worse luck than I've had recently."

"Sheila," Nancy said, "it is just possible Alonzo Rugby has not found Greystone's window at all."

The others stared at the girl detective in amazement and Sheila asked, "Whatever makes you think that?"

Nancy went on, "I shouldn't be surprised if Rugby is pulling a hoax of some kind. He's probably skillful at making stained glass and may know how to imitate the wavy effect of the old variety."

George interrupted. "Then the piece I found may be a sample of his work?"

"Yes. It's possible Rugby has put together a stained-glass window, planning to fool Sir Richard into buying the imitation—or, at least, getting the reward."

"Oh, Nancy," said Sheila, "you figure things out so magnificently. Can this mean the missing window may still be at Ivy Hall?"

"Yes, Sheila. And I suggest that we start early tomorrow on another search."

Next morning the group had only a small breakfast, then the feverish hunt began. The girls separated. Nancy decided to study the outside of the house. She walked round and round it many times, gazing at the architecture from every angle. Seeing nothing unusual, Nancy next began carefully tearing off sections of the ivy to look at the bricks closely. Presently she came to the wall of the old library. Here the bricks seemed to be of a slightly different shade from those in the rest of the building.

The young sleuth was curious. Could the missing window possibly have been in this section and bricked over? Calling the others, Nancy pointed out her find.

"Let's see what's on the other side," she suggested, excited, and they all rushed into the house.

As they entered the gloomy old library, Nancy said, "This time, Sheila, with your permission, I'd like to do a little hacking. I'll try not to tear up the walls too much."

"Go ahead," the actress said. She hardly dared hope that Nancy was going to make an important discovery.

Picking up an old fire tong, Nancy swung the handle at the plaster. Pieces began to chip off and soon there was a hole large enough to reveal what was behind it.

"A brick wall!" said Sheila. Disappointment showed in her eyes.

But Nancy was not discouraged. "If there was a window here at one time," she said, "it may have been bricked up on both sides. I can soon find out by comparing it with the wall in the next room."

In the living room Nancy chipped away some of the plaster on the wall that adjoined the suspected one. Behind the plaster were studs and lathe, with a brick wall beyond. Feeling that she had practically proved her point about the house having an inner and an outer brick wall only in a section of the library, she requested Sheila's permission to take out a few of the bricks.

"Go ahead," the actress said. "I must know if you're right."

Annette found some tools. Very cautiously Nancy used a chisel and hammer between two of the bricks. Little by little the old sand cement came away and finally she was able to lift out one of the bricks. Now she shone her flashlight inside.

Revealed were parts of a red and a blue section of leaded glass!

"The window!" Sheila cried out. "Oh, how thrilling!"

Nancy's heart was thumping wildly. "We must go immediately and try to head off Rugby before he collects any money from Sir Richard."

"How can we find Rugby?" Bess asked. "I'm sure he's not at the studio."

"I think he has a hideaway somewhere up Eddy Run," Nancy replied. "So let's get another canoe and try to locate the place."

Sheila and Annette said they would remain at Ivy Hall and guard the hidden window. With victory so close, they did not want anything to happen to it.

"Let's start!" Nancy said to Bess and George, eager to be off.

"But where are we going to find a canoe?" George reminded her.

For answer, Nancy hurried into the house and

telephoned to Mr. Honsho. She inquired if he had a canoe, and learning that he did, Nancy asked if the girls might borrow it. The Indian graciously agreed. He would have Luke take it down to the water immediately.

By the time Nancy and her friends reached the spot, the young man was waiting. The three girls thanked him, climbed into the canoe, and started.

They paddled for nearly a mile without seeing a building that might be Rugby's hide-out. Then, Nancy spotted a rather tumble-down farmhouse in a grove of trees. From the unkempt condition of the grounds, the place appeared to be uninhabited.

"Let's look," she urged. "This would make a good hide-out."

The girls beached the canoe and started up a tangled, weed-choked path to the house. Reaching it, they looked about. No one was in sight. Nancy knocked. There was no response.

"Suppose we investigate a little," George suggested, gazing at the dwelling and a small barn across a lane.

One side of the house was almost entirely obscured by high shrubbery. Nancy, Bess, and George squeezed through an opening in it, then gasped. In the wall confronting them was a stained-glass window that in every way fitted the description of the missing one!

"Oh——" Bess cried out.

Before she could say more, there was a rustle in the bushes behind the girls. Turning, they looked straight into the questioning eyes of Alonzo Rugby!

Instantly the girls were on the alert. Alonzo Rugby must not know that they suspected that the window was a copy. Nancy, smiling pleasantly, was the first to speak. "This is exquisite, isn't it?"

The man's suspicious expression relaxed. "Do you think so?" he countered.

George and Bess took their cue from Nancy and began to rave about the beautiful colors and the amazing lifelike quality of the knight and the peacock.

"Its real beauty shows up from inside the house," said Rugby enthusiastically. "Come in."

The three girls followed him inside the deserted house. From there the window looked lovely with the light shining through it. But Nancy strongly doubted that it was the old masterpiece.

Bess, with the same thought, suddenly blurted out, "Mr. Rugby, is this an old window or did you make it?"

Her words seemed to act as a signal. Without warning, a heavy-set man and a woman appeared from an adjoining room. The woman was Mrs. Dondo! They carried rope and gags with them.

"So! You little spy!" Nancy's neighbor hissed at her.

"Cut the chatter," said Rugby, who had grabbed a piece of rope. "Let's tie these kids up!"

A fierce stuggle followed, but the girls were no match for the two men and Mrs. Dondo, who fought like a tigress. Nancy, Bess, and George were quickly overpowered and securely bound. Gags were stuffed into their mouths, then the three girls were carried outside and into the barn across the lane. One by one they were lifted up a ladder and deposited in the hayloft.

Laughing scornfully, Mrs. Dondo and the men left the barn.

CHAPTER XX

The Secret of Ivy Hall

THOUGH Nancy and her friends struggled to free themselves, the effort proved hopeless. Now they squirmed through the hay, trying to get close enough together, so they could work on one another's bonds. But in their awkward positions, they could make no headway on the tight knots.

Ten minutes later, as the girls rested for a moment, they heard a car arriving. It stopped, two car doors banged, then a voice with a cheery English accent called out, "Hello there!"

From their hayloft prison the girls pictured Rugby appearing from the house. A second later, to their dismay, they heard him say, "Hello, Lord Greystone. Glad to see you."

Then they could hear Rugby being introduced by Sir Richard to a second Englishman named Mr. Peters. After chatting for a few minutes, the men apparently went inside the house.

"I *must* get loose and stop Rugby!" Nancy told herself.

She raised herself up and looked around for some other means of loosening their bonds. Suddenly she detected a scythe in a far corner of the hayloft. Dragging herself to it, Nancy began to saw through the bindings on her wrists. When her hands were free she took the gag from her mouth, then cut through the rope that bound her ankles.

"I'll have yours off in a minute," she whispered to Bess and George. When the cousins stood up, free of the ropes and gags, she said urgently, "Come on! Hurry! We must stop Rugby!"

Just as the girls started down the ladder of the haymow, Sir Richard came from the house. In a clear-cut voice he said, "Mr. Rugby, I can't tell you and your sister what this means to me. To think that at last I have found the window that belonged to my family centuries ago. Come with me to the hotel and I will give you the reward money immediately."

"I'll follow in my car," Rugby replied.

By this time Nancy was racing from the barn, with Bess and George at her heels. Disheveled, and with wisps of straw in her blond hair, she rushed up to the two visitors.

As the men looked at her in surprise, Nancy gasped. The taller of the two looked amazingly like the knight's portrait in the Patterson attic.

"Sir Richard Greystone?" she addressed him.

"Why, yes," the ruddy-complexioned man replied.

In his early fifties, he was prematurely white haired, and had a small bristly black mustache.

Rugby looked at the girls with fury in his eyes, but in a forced, pleasant tone of voice he said, "If you'll excuse us, girls, we're in a hurry."

Ignoring him, Nancy went on, "Sir Richard, I'm Nancy Drew from River Heights. You may remember my father, Carson Drew, called you a short time ago and said if the window had not been found, I was going to hunt for it. I'm sorry to intrude, but I don't think you should give Mr. Rugby the reward money until he can prove that the stained-glass window here is the one you've been looking for."

At this remark Mrs. Dondo leaped toward Nancy with the agility of a panther about to kill. "Why, you little hussy!" she shouted furiously. "Get out of here—this is none of your business!"

Her outburst shocked Sir Richard Greystone and Mr. Peters. Alonzo Rugby looked confused for a moment, then he collected his wits.

Taking hold of the Englishman's arm, he said smoothly, "Don't pay any attention to these girls. They're just smart-alecky kids. Let's go to your hotel."

But Sir Richard turned to Nancy. He said he remembered speaking to Mr. Drew and asked

Nancy to back up her accusation. Quickly the young sleuth gave a short but full account of all her suspicions regarding Rugby and his sister. Sir Richard and his friend stared in stupefaction as Nancy concluded with the girls' imprisonment in the barn.

"Mr. Rugby——" Sir Richard started to say, then he stopped and turned to look at the suspects.

Alonzo, his sister, and the other man suddenly dashed into the house. A moment later a rear door slammed. The girls raced after the fleeing trio but were too late to overtake them. They jumped into a car hidden among some trees and roared up the lane.

"We must go after them!" Nancy cried out, returning to the Englishmen.

"I'll drive!" said Mr. Peters. "Climb in!"

Nancy and her friends hopped into the rear and the car raced off. At the exit of the driveway they looked left and right and saw Rugby's car speeding to the north. Mr. Peters turned and raced after it.

About half a mile up the road, they came to a crossing. A police car with two officers in it was just reaching the intersection. Mr. Peters stopped, and Nancy quickly told the policemen the story.

The officers said they would continue the chase.

As they drove off, Nancy called, "If you find Mr. Rugby and the others, please let me know. I'm at Ivy Hall."

Nancy requested that Sir Richard drive the girls to the Patterson home. When he said he would be glad to, the young sleuth smiled. "Now I have a surprise for you."

"Haven't I had enough surprises for one day?" the Englishman asked, chuckling. "Although," he added, "I am disappointed about the window being faked."

A little dimple flickered in Nancy's cheek when she told Sir Richard that she strongly suspected the window for which he had been searching was hidden at Ivy Hall.

The man's eyebrows raised in surprise, but he said calmly, "It's worth looking into."

On reaching the mansion, Nancy introduced the Pattersons, who were astounded to hear what had happened. "What we have to show you, Sir Richard," said Sheila Patterson, "is no fake."

Nancy led him and Mr. Peters to the old library and showed them the glass behind the partition. The two men stared at it with great interest. Then Sir Richard, excited at the thought that this might be the old window that had belonged to his family, said, "Mrs. Patterson, would you permit us to take away more bricks, so that we might convince ourselves?"

"Oh, please do," Sheila replied. "I want to find out as much as you do whether this is really the old peacock window."

More tools were procured and carefully the whole group worked to uncover what was behind the bricks. Within half an hour the hind legs of a white stallion were revealed. Next came more of the horse's body, then the lower half of the knight who was riding him.

"Oh, I'm sure this is the genuine window!" Sir Richard cried out enthusiastically.

An hour later, although all the stained glass had not been uncovered, it was evident to everyone that at last Sir Richard's search had come to an end.

"And best of all," he said, "the window appears to be in good condition, even though it has been covered up. Oh, I am so grateful to you, Miss Drew."

Nancy was tingling with happiness. The strange mystery had been solved!

Sheila insisted that the weary workers relax for a while and have something to eat. With the help of Annette and Bess, she prepared a delicious meal, and the group sat on the porch to enjoy it. Presently Sir Richard, looking pensive, began to tell the history of the old window.

"In 1849 my great-grandfather, Lord Henry Greystone, passed away, leaving two sons. The elder inherited not only the family home, Grey Manor, but the bulk of his father's fortune as well. The younger son, Bruce, became angry because he had not received more and left home."

Sir Richard went on to say that Bruce had come to the United States without saying good-by to anyone. At the same time the famous stained-glass window, representing an ancestor in the crusades, had also disappeared from the great entrance hall of the family home.

"The window had been there since the thirteen hundreds," the Englishman explained. "No one was ever able to trace the window after it vanished. Since my boyhood I have been fascinated by the old story and determined to find the window if it was still in existence. I had nothing to go on but a hunch that Bruce Greystone had brought the window to this country."

He smiled at Nancy and the others, saying he would not only pay the reward money to the River Heights hospital, but that he would like to buy the window from Mrs. Patterson. Sheila gave a great gulp, hardly daring to believe her good fortune.

"It's all so thrilling!" Bess sighed.

After they finished eating, Sir Richard said, "I'd like to uncover a little more of the window."

The whole group went back to the old library and started to work. A few minutes later, Nancy

discovered a note stuck between two of the bricks.
Spreading it open, she began to read the faded
but still legible writing. Then, excited, she called
the attention of the others to it and handed the
note to Sir Richard. He read it aloud.

> *To the finder of this note:*
> *This stained-glass window is being*
> *covered up to preserve it during the*
> *war between the North and South. Our*
> *family has called itself Grayce since*
> *coming to this country from England*
> *in 1849. My father was Sir Henry*
> *Greystone. If none of my descendants*
> *is living when this window is found,*
> *will the finder please notify whoever*
> *is then Lord Greystone.*
>
> *Bruce Grayce*

Sir Richard's eyes were moist as he stared at
the note. Then, in a calm voice, he said, "This
is the last proof I needed."

As he paused, a car was heard driving up
quickly to the house. "Maybe it's the police!"
Annette said, and she rushed to the hall.

She was right. An officer came to the door and
asked if everyone in Ivy Hall would please step
outside. In his car sat Alonzo Rugby, Mrs.
Dondo, and their husky confederate.

"These three have been advised of their rights
and have made a full confession," the officer re-

ported, "but if any of you wish to question them, please go ahead."

It developed during questioning that Nancy's suspicions of Rugby and Mrs. Dondo had been correct. For some time the brother and sister had been trying to work a little racket in which they accused people of stealing letters that contained cash.

Alonzo Rugby, having read the *Continental* article about Sir Henry Greystone's offer, had decided to make an imitation window. The sight of Nancy's peacock sketch had disturbed him, because he had thought she might have found the real stained-glass window and copied the peacock on it. Later, he had changed his mind.

When Mrs. Dondo had learned through eavesdropping that Nancy was going to Virginia to hunt for the window, she had notified her brother. In order to keep the girl detective from uncovering his scheme, Rugby had first sent the fake telegram, then caused both accidents involving Susan's automobile.

"What did you hope to gain by injuring us?" Nancy asked Rugby.

"I wanted to postpone your sleuthing long enough for me to complete my job," he said. "Then when you showed up at Mr. Bradshaw's I got desperate, since I had stolen some drawings and old glass from him."

Rugby admitted wearing a stocking over his

head in the automobile and also when looking in the window at Susan's home. Then later he had knocked Nancy unconscious. Alarmed that she would learn his secret, he had entered the Patterson home with Mrs. Dondo, who had come from River Heights to help him.

"I wanted to make sure," he said, "that Nancy Drew had not found the real window and I had to do some hacking to satisfy myself."

Mrs. Dondo said sourly, "I searched the girls' baggage to see if there were any letters telling where it might be." She looked away. "And helped myself to a few articles."

"Well, I guess that concludes the questioning for the time being," the police officer spoke up. "Unmasking these swindlers must have been mighty exciting, Miss Drew."

Nancy agreed, but in many ways regreted that the intriguing mystery was ending and not just beginning. But soon she was to start on one of the most unusual adventures she had ever encountered, *The Haunted Showboat*.

After the prisoners were driven away, Nancy telephoned Seven Oaks. Susan, overjoyed to hear the good news, declared, "I'll tell the Bradshaws right away!"

A little later Nancy received a call from Mark Bradshaw himself. The artist apologized profusely for his recent unfriendly attitude and thanked her for discovering the truth about Rugby.

When Nancy rejoined the group in the Ivy Hall library, everyone was staring at the exquisite stained-glass window in silent admiration.

Presently Sir Richard said dreamily, "The knight and the peacock have traveled many miles across the ocean and will have to recross it before being restored to their original home."

At that moment the telephone rang, and Sheila went to answer it. When she came back, her eyes were shining happily. She stood in the center of the floor and said dramatically, "Never again will I say that peacocks bring me bad luck. My agent just called—I'm to have a wonderful starring part in a new Broadway play! And, Annette, you can go to college as you've been hoping!"

"Oh, I'm so happy for us," said Annette, hugging her mother. "And we'll spend vacations at Ivy Hall!"

Nancy and Bess expressed their delight at the turn in the Pattersons' fortune. George said it was great news. Then, grinning, she looked at the girl detective who had been responsible for a large part of it.

"Well, Nancy," she said, "besides solving this whole mystery and exonerating innocent people, you've even proved that peacocks are above suspicion!"

ORDER FORM

NANCY DREW MYSTERY SERIES

by Carolyn Keene

55 TITLES AT YOUR BOOKSELLER OR COMPLETE THIS HANDY COUPON AND MAIL TO:

GROSSET & DUNLAP, INC.
P.O. Box 941, Madison Square Post Office, New York, N.Y. 10010

Please send me the Nancy Drew Mystery Book(s) checked below @ $2.95 each, plus 25¢ per book postage and handling. My check or money order for $_____ is enclosed. (Please do not send cash.)

☐ 1.	Secret of the Old Clock	9501-7	
☐ 2.	Hidden Staircase	9502-5	
☐ 3.	Bungalow Mystery	9503-3	
☐ 4.	Mystery at Lilac Inn	9504-1	
☐ 5.	Secret of Shadow Ranch	9505-X	
☐ 6.	Secret of Red Gate Farm	9506-8	
☐ 7.	Clue in the Diary	9507-6	
☐ 8.	Nancy's Mysterious Letter	9508-4	
☐ 9.	The Sign of the Twisted Candles	9509-2	
☐ 10.	Password to Larkspur Lane	9510-6	
☐ 11.	Clue of the Broken Locket	9511-4	
☐ 12.	The Message in the Hollow Oak	9512-2	
☐ 13.	Mystery of the Ivory Charm	9513-0	
☐ 14.	The Whispering Statue	9514-9	
☐ 15.	Haunted Bridge	9515-7	
☐ 16.	Clue of the Tapping Heels	9516-5	
☐ 17.	Mystery of the Brass Bound Trunk	9517-3	
☐ 18.	Mystery at Moss-Covered Mansion	9518-1	
☐ 19.	Quest of the Missing Map	9519-X	
☐ 20.	Clue in the Jewel Box	9520-3	
☐ 21.	The Secret in the Old Attic	9521-1	
☐ 22.	Clue in the Crumbling Wall	9522-X	
☐ 23.	Mystery of the Tolling Bell	9523-8	
☐ 24.	Clue in the Old Album	9524-6	
☐ 25.	Ghost of Blackwood Hall	9525-4	
☐ 26.	Clue of the Leaning Chimney	9526-2	
☐ 27.	Secret of the Wooden Lady	9527-0	

☐ 28.	The Clue of the Black Keys	9528-9	
☐ 29.	Mystery at the Ski Jump	9529-7	
☐ 30.	Clue of the Velvet Mask	9530-0	
☐ 31.	Ringmaster's Secret	9531-9	
☐ 32.	Scarlet Slipper Mystery	9532-7	
☐ 33.	Witch Tree Symbol	9533-5	
☐ 34.	Hidden Window Mystery	9534-3	
☐ 35.	Haunted Showboat	9535-1	
☐ 36.	Secret of the Golden Pavilion	9536-X	
☐ 37.	Clue in the Old Stagecoach	9537-8	
☐ 38.	Mystery of the Fire Dragon	9538-6	
☐ 39.	Clue of the Dancing Puppet	9539-4	
☐ 40.	Moonstone Castle Mystery	9540-8	
☐ 41.	Clue of the Whistling Bagpipes	9541-6	
☐ 42.	Phantom of Pine Hill	9542-4	
☐ 43.	Mystery of the 99 Steps	9543-2	
☐ 44.	Clue in the Crossword Cipher	9544-0	
☐ 45.	Spider Sapphire Mystery	9545-9	
☐ 46.	The Invisible Intruder	9546-7	
☐ 47.	The Mysterious Mannequin	9547-5	
☐ 48.	The Crooked Banister	9548-3	
☐ 49.	The Secret of Mirror Bay	9549-1	
☐ 50.	The Double Jinx Mystery	9550-5	
☐ 51.	Mystery of the Glowing Eye	9551-3	
☐ 52.	The Secret of the Forgotten City	9552-1	
☐ 53.	The Sky Phantom	9553-X	
☐ 54.	The Strange Message in the Parchment	9554-8	
☐ 55	Mystery of Crocodile Island	9555-6	

SHIP TO:

NAME _____

(please print)

ADDRESS _____

CITY _____ STATE _____ ZIP _____

Printed in U.S.A. **Please do not send cash.**